MW01125597

Spells Of The Heart

By

Ellen Dugan

Spells Of The Heart
Copyright @ Ellen Dugan 2017
Cover art designed by Kyle Hallemeier
Cover image: fotolia: Andrew Kiesley
"Legacy Of Magick" logo designed by Kyle Hallemeier
Copy Editing and Formatting by Libris in CAPS

This is a work of fiction. Names, characters, businesses, organizations, places, events and incidents either are the product of the author's imagination or are used fictitiously. Any resemblance to actual persons, living or dead, events, or locales is entirely coincidental.

No part of this book may be reproduced, or stored in a retrieval system, or transmitted in any other form or by any means electronic, mechanical, photocopying, recording or otherwise without the express written permission of the publisher.

Published by Ellen Dugan

Other titles by Ellen Dugan

THE LEGACY OF MAGICK SERIES

Legacy of Magick, Book 1

Secret of the Rose, Book 2

Message of the Crow, Book 3

Beneath An Ivy Moon, Book 4

Under The Holly Moon, Book 5

The Hidden Legacy, Book 6: Featured in *Bewitched &
Beloved* with Barbara Devlin

A Legacy Of Magick Novella (October 2017)

Magick & Magnolias (Coming 2018)

THE GYPSY CHRONICLES

Gypsy At Heart, Book 1

Gypsy Spirit, Book 2 (Coming 2018)

ACKNOWLEDGMENTS

To my fabulous crew of beta readers: Michael, Ro and Shawna. Thanks for your speed reading skills, the notes, and of course for patiently listening to me while I plotted my way through this book. To Kyle for the amazing cover and for bringing Autumn to life. Thanks to Mitchell for the editing and formatting.

Finally a special thanks to Barbara who helped a sister out when she got stuck on how to give Autumn and Duncan their HEA ending.

You have bewitched me body and soul,

And I love, I love, I love you.

-Jane Austen

CHAPTER ONE

"If I cast a spell on my contractor to make him finish the reno *this* week..." I wondered out loud, "would that be considered unethical behavior?"

It was a valid question, I decided. Especially for a newer magickal practitioner like myself. Being a Witch didn't guarantee that I would stroll through life without any challenges. Sometimes it meant quite the opposite.

I pulled my car into the driveway, turned off the engine, and admired the view. The 1920's Craftsman style bungalow I'd purchased six months ago was painted a bright cheerful yellow. It had crisp white trim, a sassy red front door, and a gray roof. The house was surrounded by charming perennial gardens, and it was located conveniently next door to my family's manor home.

However, the bungalow was inconveniently, and most definitely, *haunted*.

This fact had created a never-ending horror story of delays and snafus with my renovation plans...not to mention a constant parade of spooked contractors and crews. Somewhere the old gods were laughing their asses off at me. You'd have thought I would have *foreseen* all the difficulties that I would encounter during the renovations, but no.

I was currently on my third contractor, and my bathroom tile had been on backorder for weeks. Which had been yet another frustration to add to the string of problems and postponements with completing the lower level renovation. Recalling the past few months had me pressing a hand to my nervous stomach.

My first contractor had mysteriously quit after the tear-out portion of the original kitchen and dining room had been completed. He'd left me a note saying the crew was too nervous in the house to continue working in it. So I'd gone for a second company, and I'd had to wait a month before they could get started. They managed to do the framing, wiring, drywall and the floors…but they too had walked off the job before the reno was complete. They even refunded some of my money since they wouldn't finish the job, and they refused to give me a legitimate reason why.

That's when the rumors had started around town. Every time I walked into a home improvement store, the staff gave me a wide berth. Apparently the crews had been talking, and word had gone out that the bungalow was haunted or, depending on who you asked, cursed.

Finally I'd found a third contractor from the next

town over, but once again had to wait weeks for him to schedule me in. My newest contractor, Mr. Brown, had called me at work today, notifying me that he'd installed the appliances and that the kitchen was done. I'd squealed into the phone I'd been so excited. He was beginning the tile work on the new bathroom today as well, and it should be in working order by tonight.

So, today marked an important step for me. A second working bathroom, and as of this afternoon, the kitchen renovation was complete! I couldn't wait to do some real cooking. I'd been using an upstairs bedroom as a makeshift kitchen since I'd moved in.

Crossing my fingers for luck, I climbed out of the car and walked up the short curving sidewalk to my door. The front porch steps were lined with pots of colorful annuals, and I noted as I went by that they needed a good soaking. The early September temperatures were still warm and we'd been having a dry spell. Still, the shade of the covered porch was welcoming, as was the white painted bench and small table that I'd added to create a seating area.

I let myself in, sighing in relief at the air conditioned coolness. I grinned at the empty but *clean* front room, and walked straight to the back towards the kitchen. What I saw there made me misty.

The original cabinets had been painted a crisp, clean white. I'd worked hard with the contractors, and we'd managed to add similar style cabinets to the newly expanded kitchen. They melded beautifully with the old ones. Glass-fronted cabinets shimmered to the left and right of the old farmhouse-style sink. The nickel-plated drawer pulls and cabinet handles were reproduction, sturdy, shiny and new. But they had the old *look* I'd been going for. My new white stove and dishwasher blended in exactly as I'd imagined with the lower cabinets.

The fridge was a funky retro style—but was energy efficient and brand spanking new. It shimmered white, and while it had cost me a pretty penny, seeing it in place in the kitchen made me realize I'd been correct to splurge on it.

The tile floor was new as well—there'd been no way to salvage the old floors, and it was now laid out in a soft gray and white checkerboard. The floor tiles were arranged in a diamond pattern, and they too had a retro look. The kitchen backsplash was a pale, gray subway tile with black trim, and the countertops were a solid surface composite material that was a warm smoke, slightly darker than the tile on my floors.

"It's perfect!" I said, jumping up and down in delight.

I ran around for a good five minutes trying everything out. Opening drawers and cabinets, turning on the stove, flinging the refrigerator door wide...It was everything I'd hoped for.

"Vintage pieces combined with modern convenience!" I said out loud, running my hands over the pretty cabinets. "I'm so glad we salvaged as much of the original materials as possible." I moved over to the new glass back door, delighted at the afternoon light that streamed in. I spun and took everything in from a different angle. The kitchen was large, warm and inviting, and I could hardly wait to add pops of bright color to it with my plates and red accessories.

Pumped, I went to check on my new bathroom and stopped still in the doorway. "What the hell?"

While the plumbing had been roughed in months ago, the new toilet, old-fashioned medicine cabinet, and antique sink lay on the floor, precisely where they'd been when I'd left this morning. The tiles had been delivered, but were still in their boxes, sitting inside the bare shower stall. Nothing had been installed and nothing had been done.

I grabbed my phone ready to call the contractor, but before I could, I saw a note attached with blue painter's tape to the back of the uninstalled toilet.

I yanked it free. *Dear Autumn,* it began.

The kitchen appliances have been installed, and this concludes our business here. I have refunded your money on the bathroom that we were contracted to put in—but were unable to finish. You will find your house key and my check in your mailbox, because I'm never setting foot in this house again.

By the way, you may want to call a priest.

Sincerely, Gerald Brown.

"Son of a bitch!" I shut my eyes and stomped back into the living room to face off with the unwanted, and *dead*, roommate that had become a major pain in my ass.

"Damn it Aunt Irene!" I yelled. "That's the third contractor you've scared off!"

As an answer, a light, ghostly laugh seemed to drift down the maple staircase.

"What is *wrong* with you?" I asked, tucking the note in my pocket.

Initially, I'd been surprised and then pleased when I'd learned that the bungalow had originally been built for another Bishop. First, Franklin Bishop and his wife had lived here, and eventually they'd given the home to my great-aunt Irene.

Irene, a Witch with—according to family legend—a penchant for less than ethical spell-casting, had lived in the bungalow alone until the late 1980's. After she'd passed away, the house had been sold to a different family.

When the house had gone up for sale earlier this year, I had jumped at the chance to have it, thus putting the bungalow back in Bishop family hands after almost thirty years of different owners. *I mean how perfect was that?* I loved the architecture, the gardens connected with the grounds of the manor, I had my own place—and it was right next door to my family!

And yes, I'd grasped pretty quickly that I wasn't *alone* in the house. Not only am I a Witch and a Seer, I'm also a psychic sensitive. Which means I can *see* the past, present and future...and I'm also able to see, hear and interact with ghosts stuck in this realm.

Whether I like it or not.

But the idea hadn't bothered me. I've dealt with some pretty incredible things since I moved to William's Ford a few years ago.

However, at the moment, if it would have been possible, I'd have throttled my dead relative. I marched to the front door, yanked it open and checked the mailbox on the outside of the house. Sure enough, an envelope was inside. I tore it open and found my spare key and a check from Mr. Brown.

I shut the door behind me and sat on the floor of my empty living room in my purple cotton sundress, feeling frustrated, angry and disappointed. I dropped my head in my hands and let a few tears fall. "I am so angry with you right now," I said, figuring she was listening. "Aunt Irene, why are you doing this to me?"

I sat there glaring across the room at the door of that unfinished bathroom, and the scent of lilacs wafted through the air. That was Aunt Irene's calling card of sorts. "Maybe I can tile the bathroom myself." *I watched those shows on HGTV. It didn't look so hard...*

Suddenly, something skidded across the floor. I jolted when an old, faded red cookbook came to a stop directly in front of me. I recognized it instantly as the one I'd found hidden behind a panel in the kitchen pantry months ago.

"What is that supposed to mean?" I asked crossly.

I waited, but nothing else happened. I picked up the

old red book and frowned at it. "I had this packed up," I muttered, wondering how she'd managed to get a physical object downstairs. "Is there a recipe in here for banishing Witch-ghosts?" I flipped through the pages like I was searching for one. "Because if there is, I'm gonna use it."

As if in answer, the book fell open to a recipe entitled: *Banish Bad Vibes Brownies.*

"Funny." Shaking my head, I stood and went into the kitchen. I decided to put the old cookbook inside the glass-fronted cabinet for now. As I closed the cabinet, I caught movement reflected in the seeded glass. I didn't jump, but held very still and studied the figure in the glass. It was an older woman, striking, with salt and pepper hair. She was wearing a simple blue dress and was smiling at me.

I moved slowly. Even though I knew she wouldn't physically be there when I turned around, I looked for her anyway. The house was silent, and I was alone. "Is allowing me to finally see you, a way of saying you're sorry?" I asked.

There was no answer.

A knock on the backdoor had me clutching my chest and spinning in surprise. My cousin Holly stood on the back porch, wearing shorts and a pink tank top, her red-gold curls exploding all around her face. She waved at me through the glass door. I flipped the lock on the door and let her in.

"I came to see the kitchen and bath. Give me the

tour!" She smiled and gave me a hug.

"The kitchen is done, but the contractors walked off the job. Again." I pulled the note out of my pocket and handed it to her.

Holly read the note and snorted with laughter. "I'm sorry," she said, trying to maintain a sober expression. "I'm not laughing *at* you. But this line about calling a priest...that's funny."

"What the hell am I gonna do, Holly?" I said. "The reno has taken twice as long as it should have because of all the delays and Aunt Irene's ghostly antics."

"I wonder why she's trying to hold things up." Holly walked over to check the bathroom for herself.

"Where in the world am I going to find a contractor who she can't scare off the job?" I ran a hand through my hair. "What am I supposed to do, put in the contract, 'Please don't pay any mind to the ghost of the old Witch who used to live here'?"

"I have a suggestion," Holly said, coming back to stand by me.

"Lay it on me," I said, "because at this point I'll consider anything."

Holly's eyes met mine. "There is a contractor we both know, who could roll with whatever Aunt Irene threw at him."

"No," I said, realizing where she was heading. "Aw, hell no."

"Yes," Holly said just as firmly. "Autumn, you need to call Duncan Quinn."

***

Holly planted herself in my house, insisting on helping me set up the kitchen, and she wouldn't budge. It always surprised me how stubborn my cousin could be. She'd given me a hand hauling my dishes and accessories up from the basement where I'd stored them, and we got to work. While I wiped down all the cabinets and started to place my dishes where I wanted them, Holly went and gathered up the food from the makeshift kitchen and brought it downstairs and tucked it into the pantry.

She'd even transferred the items from the mini fridge into the new big refrigerator in the kitchen, and systematically shot down every reason I could come up with for *not* calling my former lover to have him finish the renovations on my house.

We walked across the back yard towards the detached garage that I'd been using for storage for the past few months and went to fetch my antique kitchen table and chairs. My temper was starting to unravel from the quiet, polite argument she'd been hitting me with for the past hour. *Stubborn red-haired Witch,* I thought crossly.

"Said the pot to the cauldron." Holly sniffed at me as I shoved the garage door up.

"What?" Thrown by the non sequitur, I blinked.

"I'm *not* the one who's stubborn." Holly tossed her

curls over her shoulder. "You are."

I huffed out a breath. "I didn't say anything."

"You don't have to." She poked me in the ribs. "You still project your thoughts and feelings when you are angry or upset."

"I'm *not* angry."

Holly rolled her eyes. "Try that lie again with someone who isn't an empath."

I stepped into the garage and pulled the dust sheet off the red and white enamel table with the chrome legs. "I'm stressed out," I said. "The renovations should have been completed months ago. And I'm very disappointed that the lower bathroom isn't completed."

Holly went to the opposite side of the table and lifted. "So, call the *one* contractor who wouldn't bat an eye at an interfering ghost on the premises."

We lifted the table and began hauling it across the lawn. "I haven't seen Duncan in months."

"Not since the big museum fundraiser this spring." Holly smiled. "Where he watched you the entire evening."

I stopped at the base of the back porch steps. "No he didn't."

Holly merely raised her eyebrows. "Yes, he did."

"No he didn't," I argued, "and I would know, because I kept an eye—" I cut myself off.

"Because you kept an eye on him yourself all night long," Holly said.

"I kept an eye on *all* the Drakes that night," I

countered. "Especially your arch nemesis, Leilah Drake Martin." We carefully flipped the table on its side and began to maneuver it up the steps.

"Everyone's favorite little psychopath." Holly grunted as we went up the steps.

"Any rumbles out of her lately?"

"No, not really," Holly said. "Nothing I can't handle anyway."

"Watch the table legs," I warned, as we eased the table through the doorway. Once we were in, we righted the table and set it in place. "Oh, wow, this does look good." I ran my hand proudly over the enamel top of the table.

Holly held open the back door. "Let's go get your chairs and set it all up."

We trooped back across the yard and picked up the four mismatched wooden chairs that I'd painted all in the same shade of candy apple red. I rolled the garage door down and followed Holly back inside.

"Any preference as to which chair goes where, Autumn?"

"Nope." I set two chairs in place, as Holly did, and stepped back to admire. "There," I said. "It's finally starting to look like a home."

"A home of your very own." Holly adjusted a chair. "The table goes well with the pendant farmhouse light fixture I got for you."

"It really does," I sighed happily.

"It sure would be nice if the *entire* downstairs was

finished." Holly stuck her tongue in her cheek.

I narrowed my eyes at her. "Subtle, Blondie. Real subtle."

"I could call Duncan for you," Holly volunteered.

"He's probably too busy, anyway."

A banging on the glass back door saved me from further argument. My three and a half year old nephew, Morgan John, had his face pressed up against the glass and was looking in. "Hi!" He grinned at me and Holly. "Mommy said I could come visit!"

Quickly, I went to the door to let him in. "Hi MJ." I looked out over the yard and gave a wave to his mother, Lexie. She smiled and went back inside the manor.

"I came through the garden. Like you said I could." Morgan hugged my legs.

"That's exactly right." I patted his shoulder.

"I like the new gate," he said. "The flowers are getting big!"

I'd had a six-foot section of the metal privacy fence that had once separated the properties taken down, thus creating an entrance from the manor's yard to my bungalow. It was a huge hit with my nephew and made it much faster popping back and forth from my house to the manor. While there wasn't a formal gate per se, that's what we'd started calling the opening in the fence.

"The moonflowers will start blooming soon," I said, speaking of the vines I'd planted in the spring.

Morgan's eyes lit on the table and chairs. "Which

chair is mine?" He wanted to know.

"Actually," I said, going to the pantry, "I thought *this* might be your special chair." I pulled out a tall, vintage step stool chair and placed it next to the counter.

Fascinated, he climbed up the steps and sat on the seat of the red metal chair. "This is *my* chair. I'm up high. I can help cook."

"You'll be the perfect height in that." Holly nodded.

"'Cause I'm a big boy now," Morgan said, pleased with himself. "Babies can't cook."

Holly hid a grin. "No, they can't." My nephew was still a little bent out of shape by the arrival of his three month old sister, Belinda.

"Tomorrow," I told him, "you and I can bake some cookies in my new kitchen. How about that?"

"Okay!" He banged the heels of his tennis shoes on the chrome legs of the step stool.

As soon as I get to the grocery store and stock up, I thought, and made a mental note to get to the store tonight before Violet came over to visit.

"This is my chair, 'Reen," Morgan said, waving at an empty corner of the kitchen.

All the hair rose on the back of my neck. From the day I'd taken possession of the house, Morgan had been having conversations with someone he called 'Reen. Aka- *Great Aunt Irene.* "Hello, Aunt Irene. What do you think of the new kitchen?" I said conversationally.

The glass fronted cabinet where I'd stashed her

cookbook slowly opened.

"She likes it," my nephew said very seriously.

"Aunt Irene," Holly said in the same casual tone. "Autumn needs to finish the renovation. What do you think about Duncan Quinn coming over to the bungalow to do the work?"

"Holly!" I hissed at her, embarrassed that she'd bring that up in front of Morgan—who was sure to repeat it to his father, my brother, Bran.

"'Reen is smiling, Holly." He started to laugh and clap his hands. "She didn't like the other guys."

I tossed up my hands, and Holly started to grin. Morgan glanced from Holly to me, trying to figure out what was so funny.

***

"Brown sugar, vanilla, chocolate chips..." Intent on my list, I was focused on the baking aisle at the grocery store. It was so wonderful to be able to stock up and buy real cooking and baking supplies. Stopping in front of the chocolate chip display, I pushed my glasses back up my nose. Eyeballing the dark chocolate chips, I grabbed two bags and chucked them in. I pushed my cart forward and was so busy making sure I hadn't forgotten anything—that I ran my grocery cart right into the butt of another shopper.

"Oof!" a male voice sounded.

I yanked the cart back and my purse hit the floor.

"Sorry!" I glanced up. "I wasn't watching where I was —"

"We really have to stop meeting like this," Duncan Quinn said.

It took me a moment to find my voice. *Damn, he looked wonderful.* Duncan's jeans were torn at the knee, and his t-shirt stretched over a nicely built chest...and if I wasn't mistaken he was more ripped since the last time I'd seen him. His blue eyes were clear, and he appeared relaxed and happy.

In fact, my ex looked better than ever.

"Of all the baking aisles in town, you had to be in mine," I grumbled.

He grinned at that. "Hello, Autumn."

I bent down and grabbed my purse. "Sorry about the collision. Are you okay?" I slung the purse strap over my shoulder and stood up straight.

"I'm fine. How are you?" he asked.

"Fine," I answered far too quickly. "I'm doing fine.

He considered my cart. "Looks like you're going to be baking cookies." He picked up a bag of chocolate chips for himself from the grocery shelf and added them to a cart that held beer, cheese, and fresh fruit.

"Uh, yeah." I did my best not to fidget. "I promised Morgan we'd bake cookies together. Sort of a ceremonial first time to use the new kitchen appliances celebration."

"I thought your reno had started in April?"

"It did. I hit a few snags along the way."

"Six months is more than a few snags." Duncan frowned. "What happened?"

"Well hey, this has been great running into you again, but I really have to go." I flashed a smile, prayed it appeared sincere and maneuvered the cart around him. The last thing I needed was Duncan Quinn being all casually friendly and chatty...not to mention looking sexy as hell.

I zipped around the corner and headed up the cereal aisle. I stared at the boxes blindly. *Had Holly called him?* I wondered. *In the years since we'd broken up I'd rarely bumped into him in public...Not counting that night back in March when I'd gotten a little toasted and he'd assisted Holly in getting me to the car, and I'd drunkenly told him he was the best lover I'd ever had.*

I cringed, blew out a breath, and concentrated on acting casual and sophisticated. I strolled down the next two aisles without tripping or running into anyone else, and didn't put a single thing in my cart. Somewhere around the toilet paper aisle I managed to get ahold of myself. I stared at my list, realizing that I'd missed a few items while I'd been so busy acting nonchalant.

"At least I was able to protect my thoughts from him." I muttered to myself. *God! How embarrassing would that have been if he could have picked up on my admiring the way he looked?* I'd learned the hard way how to block off my thoughts where men were concerned. After all, I'd gotten a crash course while dating that gorgeous Creole man, Rene.

I tucked my hair behind my ear, backtracked, finished up my shopping and rolled all of my purchases out to my car. I'd begun to load the bags in the trunk when Duncan suddenly appeared next to my cart. I didn't flinch, but it was a very near thing. "Hello, Duncan."

"Let me help you." Without waiting for my assent he started loading the groceries in the trunk.

"Thanks." I nodded and loaded a few more bags. *He was simply being friendly,* I told myself. Then I snuck a peek at his butt as he leaned in to place the bags in the trunk. *Lord and Lady,* I thought. *He still had a nice backside.*

"Restocking the kitchen are we?" he asked cheerfully.

I jerked guiltily and reminded myself that he was a telepath. If I thought too 'loud' in his direction, especially when I was standing close to him, he would probably pick it up. "Yeah," I attempted to answer in the same casual way he had. "Now that I have a working kitchen again, I'm looking forward to actually cooking a meal as opposed to nuking something in the microwave."

"I'll bet." He set the last bag in and shut the trunk for me.

"So what were you doing grocery shopping?" I asked. "Doesn't the staff at the Drake mansion do that for you?"

He snorted at that. "I help out the housekeeper

sometimes, but Mrs. J. doesn't buy my beer. Besides, Leilah asked me to pick up a few things, she's baking for a Sorority fundraiser or something."

And with his words, reality dampened my appreciation for his masculine charms. "I didn't realize you and your cousin were so close."

"Leilah's okay. She's been trying to do better."

"How nice." I pushed the cart to a nearby cart round up. Considering what had gone down between Holly and Leilah, this topic of conversation was doomed to certain failure.

Duncan was still standing next to my car, waiting for me. "Autumn, you know I'd never condone the magickal violence that happened between Leilah and Holly."

"Yes, I know," I said, meeting his eyes. "Our families have a complicated history, and honestly neither side is blameless."

We stood in that busy parking lot, only a few feet apart, but the distance between us was huge.

"I've missed you," he said quietly.

Those three little words had my breath catching in my throat. For some crazy reason I suddenly ached to hold him. Just hold him. Even though he appeared fit, healthy and happy, somehow he still seemed in need of a hug. Which made me feel slightly guilty for eyeballing his butt.

"Well, I'd better get going. Violet is coming over tonight." I took a deliberate step back. It was nice to see you, Duncan," I said. "Take care of yourself."

"You too," he said.

I got in my car and steered towards the exit, telling myself not to look back.

I did anyway, and felt a little tug at my heart when I saw him watching me as I drove away.

CHAPTER TWO

I barely managed to get my groceries put away before there was a knock on my front door. I shut the pantry, took a quick glance around the kitchen to check that everything was in place, and went to answer the door.

"Hello!" I smiled at Violet O'Connell as she stood on my front porch. Her blonde hair was long and dyed a gorgeous purple ombre at the bottom. She was wearing a t-shirt in her trademark color of purple, and her arms were full with a shopping bag and a blooming cyclamen plant in a woven basket.

"Hey!" She grinned and handed me the plant. "Happy new kitchen! I hope you don't mind, but I brought a friend along that I'd like you to meet."

"Sure," I said, taking the basket. As Violet stepped inside the bungalow, I caught sight of a petite and curvy young woman. I estimated her to be a couple inches over five feet tall, and her platinum hair fell in waves to her shoulders.

"Hey there." Chocolate brown eyes twinkled up at me. "I'm Candice Jacobs." She wore a flowing top in fuchsia, denim walking shorts, and had a small silver pentagram around her neck. She also held a platter filled with what appeared to be bonbons—on lollipop sticks.

"Jacobs?" I asked. "Any relation to Oliver Jacobs?"

"Oliver Jacobs is my dad," she said. "My father and your dad, Arthur, were first cousins. We share a great-grandmother. Which makes us second, or maybe third cousins."

I recognized her as a fellow Witch, both by the jewelry and her personal energy. "It's nice to meet more family," I said. "*And* you have chocolate. Come on in."

I felt a little buzz of power as Candice crossed the threshold. Taking that as confirmation, I let the storm door shut behind her and stepped down into the living room where Violet stood waiting.

"When does your living room furniture get delivered?" Violet asked.

"This weekend," I told her. "Let's head on through to the kitchen." Leading the way, I chose a sunny spot on the kitchen counter for the plant and set it down.

Candice slid her platter on the table. "This is an awesome space for cooking and baking." She went to the stove and practically cooed over the new range.

"Candice is a baker." Violet grinned, pulling a bottle of wine and a corkscrew out of the shopping bag.

"Like your father?" I asked Candice as she opened

the oven door and peered inside.

"Yes, and no." Candice closed the oven. "I worked at the doughnut shop while I earned an associate degree at the community college. Then I went off to culinary school in Chicago and got a second degree with a focus on Pastry Arts."

I smiled at her. "I'm friends with Shannon, your sister in law."

"Yeah, she mentioned you. Told me we should meet."

"Wine glasses?" Violet asked.

"To the right of the sink," I answered her.

"Candice is opening up her own business next door to the flower shop," Violet announced as she brought three of my wine glasses to the table.

"Oh yeah? Are you gonna give Oliver a run for his money?" I asked.

Candice laughed and pulled out a kitchen chair. "He'd disown me if I even *thought* about competing with Blue Moon Bakery." She sat and pushed the platter in front of me. "My culinary talents and focus tends to run in a different direction than doughnuts and muffins."

"What are these?" I asked, gazing at the pretty little candy-coated spheres. They were gorgeous. Some had swirls of glitter going around them and others were decorated with different colored sprinkles.

"Cakepops." Candice winked at me. "Red velvet dipped in white chocolate and yellow cake dipped in dark chocolate." She nudged the platter closer. "Try one."

I eyeballed the dozen cakepops before me. "They're almost too pretty to eat."

"Nonsense," Candice said.

Violet handed me a glass of wine. "No worries, I brought a dessert wine."

I snorted out a laugh and chose a cakepop covered in white chocolate. I leaned back in my chair and took a bite. "Oh my goddess," I said with my mouth full.

Violet snatched a dark chocolate covered cakepop and bit in. "Yeah, you could say she's got the magick touch." She gave a happy sigh and closed her eyes. "Kitchen Witches are the very best friends to have."

"Aw, thanks, Violet." Candice chose one for herself. "Anyway, I'm going to open up a specialty shop next month. Cupcakes and cakepops, some artisan chocolates..."

"That's great!" I took a sip of the wine.

"With brides wanting to have more options for their receptions, cakepops, cupcakes and dessert bars are popular for weddings these days," Candice explained. "What started out as a little side business, has taken on a life of its own."

Listening as she discussed her new business, I chose a dark chocolate covered cakepop next. "Wow," I managed after sampling it. "If this is any indication, you're going to be a very busy woman."

Candice grinned. "Thanks."

Violet gobbled down her cakepop. "Brides usually ask me for recommendations for wedding desserts. The other day I had someone ask me if I knew anyone who did miniature pies. Anyway, Candice, being as we're gonna be neighbors, I figured we could cross-promote."

"That would be great!" Candice bounced in her chair. "Did you know, Dad has actually started doing doughnut cakes for weddings?"

"Doughnut cakes?" I asked her.

"Yeah." Candice leaned forward. "Imagine a huge pyramid built of all different sorts of doughnuts. It's a really fun option for brunch weddings."

"That *is* a cool idea." I nodded. "But I gotta tell you after sampling these, if I ever took the plunge; I'd do cakepops at my wedding reception. These are great."

"Thinking of weddings?" Violet asked with a raised brow.

"No." I washed down the dessert with wine. "No, I'm not seeing anyone." *You saw Duncan at the grocery store.* My inner monologue argued back.

I firmly ignored that.

"I'm not seeing anyone either," Candice sighed. "Besides, I've got a business to open and I want it ready to roll by the end of October. I don't have time for romantic relationships."

"Ditto." Violet topped off her wine. "I've had my heart broken once. I don't care for a repeat performance."

"Well then, who needs men?" I raised my glass.

"Here's to friends, old and new, and to chocolate."

"Blessed be." Candice tapped her glass to mine.

"*Sláinte*." Violet tapped her glass to ours. "Now give me the grand tour, Autumn. I want to see what you've done with the place."

I spent a pleasant evening with Violet and Candice. Candice had us howling with laughter as she regaled us with tales from culinary school. I waved goodbye to them from my front porch a few hours later and sat on the bench to enjoy the sunset and the cooler evening air.

As dusk fell, I sat listening to the cicadas and told myself I wasn't lonely. *I had family right next door, and friends. I'd even made a new friend tonight.* "Besides, I'm not ready to love again," I muttered, staring up at the moon. A shooting star zipped across the sky and I jolted. Hoping that the universe hadn't taken my words as a challenge, I stood, preparing to head back inside, when a plaintive little meow stopped me.

I spun around and searched the front porch. Half expecting Merlin, the family's black cat, to have dropped by for a visit, I went down the front steps and called for him. "Kitty, kitty," I said softly.

I followed the meows around to the side of the house. The farther I walked, the more I realized that it wasn't Merlin. Concerned, I kept searching. "Where are you?" I pulled my cell phone out of my back pocket, hit the flashlight app, and shined the light in the shadowy parts of the gardens. I walked closer to the opening in the fence and noticed with some surprise that the first of the moonflowers had started to open. I'd taken a step forward when I felt something brush across my bare foot.

I glanced down, and a young, scrawny cat with dirty white fur peered up at me.

"*Meow*," the small cat cried, rubbing against my ankle.

"Oh!" I scooped it up and felt it shiver. "Where did you come from?"

The skinny cat burrowed into my arms and my heart was lost. I had a hunch that it had been on its own for a while. I carried it into the house and took it straight into the kitchen. I got out a little bowl and filled it full of water. I sat down on the floor and put the cat in front of the bowl.

The cat lapped at the water. Now in the light I could see her clearly. She was far too thin. Female, I figured, as it was a calico. Scruffy patches of orange and black were scattered in patches across the dirty white fur. Her front legs were mostly white and the top of her head and back were a mixture of the three colors. *The poor thing.*

The little cat finished drinking and turned around and climbed back into my lap. I carefully pet her silky ears and grinned when I felt her purr. I pulled out my cell phone, aimed it, and took her picture.

I sent a quick text to Holly: *Look what I found. Can you bring me over a little cat food?*

OMG! On my way. Holly replied.

Holly let herself in the back door a few moments later. She carried a plastic baggie filled with dry food. "Where'd you find it?" she wanted to know.

"Around back, under the moonflowers."

Holly pulled a saucer out of the cabinets and came over. She sat down slowly and poured a bit of the dry food on the saucer.

The cat's head popped up when Holly poured the kibble on the saucer. Holly gently set the saucer down on the floor, and the cat climbed off my lap and went straight to the food.

"She's hungry," Holly said. "The poor thing's been on her own for a while."

"That's what I thought," I said. "I'll have to ask around and see who she belongs to."

"I think she belongs with you." Holly ran a fingertip across the cat's back.

"I suppose I should take her to a vet, and get her checked out."

"Dr. Barron has evening hours on Friday," Holly said, speaking of the family's vet. "The animal hospital would be open. Let me give them a call, and find out if they can see us."

Which is how I found myself being driven across town by my cousin with the foundling cat wrapped in a towel.

We were ushered into a treatment room and the doctor came right in. We talked for a bit, and after testing the young cat for feline leukemia, which was thankfully negative, the vet administered liquid vitamin drops and started her on vaccinations. Dr. Barron estimated the short-haired cat to be under a year old. The cat wasn't micro chipped but was in fact a spayed, declawed female. Basically the cat was undernourished, but other than being dirty, she was surprisingly okay.

"How could someone dump her?" I wondered.

"It happens," the vet said, sadly. "It's lucky you found her when you did."

"I'll take her in," I said to Dr. Barron. "She's not going to a shelter."

"Congratulations." Holly put an arm around my shoulders. "You're a pet parent."

I filled out the paperwork for the animal clinic and bought some dry cat food from them. I also made arrangements to bring the cat back for a follow up visit. Holly and I were on the road again within an hour, making a pit stop to get some cat shampoo and litter box supplies.

We hauled everything inside and it was after ten by the time we'd managed to give the cat a warm bath in the deep kitchen sink. We tried to be as gentle as possible, and she suffered through it with a few very unhappy yowls. That stopped once we had her out of the water and wrapped up in an old towel. As we dried her off I found that she had a black half moon shaped spot on her left flank.

"Huh, check that out." I showed the marking to Holly.

Holly patted the cat on the head. "If that's not a sign that she's meant to be a Bishop cat, I don't know what is."

Lexie came over from the manor with a heating pad, and we put it on the lowest setting. Wrapping the cat up in another dry towel, I set her on it. The little cat yawned so big that she fell over and promptly went to sleep.

Lexie smiled down at the calico. "What are you going to name her?" she asked.

"Between the mark on her leg, and finding her under the moonflowers," I said. "I was thinking about calling her Luna."

***

Luna lived up to her name by being wide awake at night. I'd started out by having her in a little box that included the heating pad and a towel. I set the box in my bedroom, and a litter pan in another corner. I figured the cat would be exhausted from the day and sleep through the night...

And why I'd ever thought that would work was currently beyond me. As soon as I'd clicked off the light, she started to meow and explore the room.

I called to her softly and the meows stopped. A moment later I felt her jump up on the bed. I stayed very still and waited to see what she would do. She walked gingerly up along my side and sat, staring at me. I reached out slowly to pet her and the cat leaned into it, and began to purr. I hadn't expected her to be so friendly so soon, but Luna slowly climbed up on me and stretched out on my chest. I gently ran my hand over her head and she began to knead and purr. I fell asleep with the light still on and Luna purring away.

I woke up at sunrise to the cat peering down into my face. Large olive green eyes stared at me, and I started to laugh. Then I thought about whether or not she'd used the litter box and hurried to get her to it. While Luna scratched around her pan, I double checked and was relieved to see that she hadn't left me any presents in the bedroom.

I sat on the side of the bed, swinging my feet and waited while the cat went about her business. Once she finished, she hopped out and scrambled across the area rug. She made a jump for the bed and strolled over like she'd always lived here. Luna appeared to be proud of herself as she climbed directly into my lap.

"So, you're here one night and you already rule the roost?" I gave her a little pat.

"*Meow*," Luna replied, and nudged her head under my hand.

"Come on cat," I said with a large yawn. "Let's go get breakfast." I called to her and she followed me down the stairs to the kitchen.

While Luna explored the kitchen, I ran around and made sure all of the doors to the unfinished bathroom, basement, and hall closet were shut. Then I panicked over the fireplace and double-checked to make sure the cat couldn't nose her way past the screen.

Luna scampered across the empty living room chasing the rainbows that the prisms in the front window had created on the hardwood floors. After a little while I picked her back up and carried her to the downstairs litter box, hoping to remind her where it was. I backed up and let her nose around. When she hopped out, she scampered back to the living room and was back to chasing rainbows.

Sitting at my kitchen table, I ate breakfast and watched Luna play. I suddenly realized that by adopting a foundling cat my master plan for the weekend had been completely demolished. My new living room furniture was scheduled to be delivered by noon, *and* I needed to cat proof my entire house.

A knock on the kitchen door had me turning. Lexie stood on the back porch, holding Belinda. I jumped up to let them in. "Morning." Lexie walked in. "How'd last night go?"

"Luna didn't settle down until I let her sleep on the bed with me." I yawned.

"Sucker," Lexie said. She sat at my table, shifting the baby to her lap. Lexie handed the baby a bright yellow rattle, and Belinda shook it once and chucked it on the floor.

"Yeah, yeah." I retrieved the rattle, and focused on my niece. "And how are you this morning, Miss Belinda?"

Belinda blinked at me with big blue eyes and smiled. She was wearing a sort of stretchy baby headband in pink, and my niece was mostly bald. What little hair that she did have was growing in to be the same dark blonde as her mother's. The baby's hands waved as she worked up to a sort of squealing sound.

"Tell me all about it," I said to the baby. I shifted my attention to her mama. "You want some coffee or tea?"

Lexie asked for tea so I started a pot. While we visited, Luna scrambled into the kitchen and pounced on the laces of my sister-in-law's tennis shoes.

"So," Lexie said, "Holly tells me you're needing yet another contractor to finish up the new bathroom."

I set a mug in front of her. "She thinks I should call Duncan."

Lexie sipped at her tea. "Maybe you should."

I sat across from her. "Considering our past history, I'm not sure that's such a good idea."

"You're hiring him to work on the bathroom, not asking him to go on a romantic cruise to the Caribbean," she pointed out dryly.

"What if me hiring him to work on the house gives him the wrong idea?" I argued.

"And what if it gets your renovations finally complete?" she countered. "Besides, according to Morgan, Aunt Irene didn't like the other guys."

"Har-har."

Lexie's expression changed. She stopped smiling and leaned forward a bit. "What happened between you and Duncan when he was under the influence of the grimoire...well, it changed the both of you."

"I know," I said. "It's been four years since that night we fought. And almost three years since he asked me to see him as he truly was—once he was free of the manipulative magick that his mother had worked on him."

"He went through hell." She nodded. "After facing off with Rebecca myself, it has made me a little more sympathetic to Duncan."

I reached across the table for her hand. Lexie had never spoken to me about the details of her battle with Rebecca Drake-Quinn.

"I'm a competent Witch, and trained as a police officer." Lexie paused for a moment. "I'm a damn good shot, and I know how to defend myself against physical attacks, *and* magickal ones. But I'll be honest. Rebecca came at me hard, and from out of nowhere."

"Lexie," I began.

"No, hear me out." Lexie shook her head. "That night it took *everything* I had to protect Morgan."

"She'd gone after Morgan?" I asked, horrified at the thought.

"She tried." Lexie's expression was fierce. "She paid for it." Lexie ran her hand over her daughter's head. "That night I did what I could to draw her away from him, and even now, three years later, it's still hard for me to describe the sheer amount of power she was throwing down."

"I know exactly what you mean," I said.

I flashed back to when I'd faced off with Rebecca myself. While Lexie had lain unconscious in the hospital, the family had rallied around her. I'd figured out where to find the grimoire and had snuck off to end the conflict once and for all. Once at the Drake mansion, I'd discovered that Aunt Faye had been a victim of Rebecca's manipulations, and that Duncan was completely under his mother's magickal influence as well.

Luna came over and pawed at my leg. I picked up the cat and held her for comfort. Much as Lexie was doing with the baby. "I'd done my best standing up to her too," I said, shaking my head, "but in the end it was Thomas Drake who shielded me from his sister's magick."

Belinda gurgled happily and banged her rattle against the table. The noise surprised her.

"I still have nightmares," I admitted.

"You do?" Lexie frowned.

"Yeah, it's sort of like a replay of the battle. Getting blown across the room, and hitting my head. Julian Drake working healing magick to get me on my feet, so Aunt Faye and I could escape the mansion. The three of us stumbling out in the storm. The lightning striking the roof." I stopped and cleared my throat. "Thomas left Rebecca to die in that fire, and yet he still managed to drag Duncan outside."

Lexie sighed. "Who would've ever guessed that old

man Drake had a heroic side?"

"It couldn't have been easy. Duncan was so far under Rebecca's thrall that he was like a zombie." I shuddered. "He would have died if not for his uncle."

"None of the survivors walked away from that night without a few scars, physically or emotionally," Lexie said solemnly. "Not the Drakes, and certainly not any of us."

"A few weeks after the Grand Coven assembled, Duncan asked me for another chance. He told me that he'd wait for me," I said, sitting back in my chair.

"You obviously decided not to." Lexie frowned.

"I was seeing Rene at the time," I reminded her.

"You're leaving something out." Lexie narrowed her eyes. "Spill it."

"Duncan told me that he loved me. That he'd be waiting for me to come back to him, and he kissed me."

Lexie said nothing, but gave my hand a sympathetic squeeze.

I felt my throat grow tight. "It was the first time he'd ever said that he loved me, Lexie. And then he stepped back and let me go."

"Wow." Lexie whistled.

"That was almost three years ago, and I've never had anything hurt like that."

"Okay, now I understand why you'd be hesitant of having him in the house working for you as a contractor."

"It's not so much that he is my ex. It's more that I

don't want to—"

"Lead him on," Lexie said.

"Exactly."

"Have you heard from Rene Rousseau lately?" Lexie asked in a completely different tone.

"No," I said flatly. "He appears to have plenty to keep him entertained these days." *The gorgeous Creole man I'd once dated seemed to be getting along quite nicely without me,* I thought, and allowed a squirming Luna to hop down.

"Are you okay?" Lexie asked.

I smirked. "It's a horrible thing to see your former boyfriend all over social media, and in the company of supermodels."

"I'm *still* surprised that he left William's Ford and relocated." Lexie let go of my hand and sipped her tea. "Were you in love with Rene?" she asked casually.

"To paraphrase Lady Gaga," I said, "it wasn't love. It was however—a damn good illusion."

Lexie winced. "Ouch."

"I don't know why I was so surprised when all was said and done." I tried to make myself relax. "Call it an illusion or a glamour, that sexual sort of magickal fascination was Rene Rousseau's specialty."

"I never thought about it that way," Lexie said. "But as a model his whole career was all about his looks and his ability to sell a product or to captivate women's imaginations."

"I figured out a few months ago that he literally fed

off the interest of other women whenever they were attracted to him."

"You're saying that—"

"He wasn't able to take energy from me." I cut her off. "He always claimed that I did it to him though, when we were...intimate. And that it made him feel worn down."

"I call bullshit!" Lexie jerked forward, and the baby bounced happily on her mother's lap.

"Agreed."

"I had no idea," Lexie said. "I thought you were happy together."

"I was content, and he made me feel safe," I admitted. "Our sex life wasn't the best, but for a long time I figured maybe that was all a Witch like me would be able to have."

"Contentment and safety? That is the biggest bunch of crap I've ever heard in my life," Lexie stated firmly. "So what if you're strong willed? You deserve passion! And by the way, a *real* man would find that..." she trailed off as I began to smile.

"I get it," I said. "And thanks for the pep talk."

"I hadn't realized you'd been keeping so much to yourself." Lexie bounced Belinda on her lap when she began to squirm. "You could have come to me, if you needed an ear."

"Well you've been a little busy with Morgan, and now Belinda," I pointed out.

Lexie stood and walked around the table. "You're

family. If you need me all you have to do is call."

I stood and gave her and the baby a hug. "Will do."

***

The living room furniture was delivered after lunch. I corralled the cat in the large walk-in pantry while the front door was open, and tried not to feel guilty while the men were setting up the plush gray sectional. The matching storage ottoman was set in place and I did my best not to jump up and down in excitement. After six months of not having a couch, I was thrilled to finally own living room furniture.

Once the movers left, I rushed to open the pantry door. "Sorry," I said as Luna strutted past me with her black and orange tail held high. She sat on the brick hearth, surveying the changes to the room. I hurried to my living room closet to take out two lamps and their shades. I'd also been storing burnt orange throw pillows, and a soft plush throw in the same warm shade. A small box of framed family photos joined my stack of accessories.

I went out to the garage and hauled in the retro end tables one at a time. Finally, I was able to set the lamps in place and put on the final touches. I unwrapped the framed photos, while Luna sat beside me sniffing at the contents of the box.

One by one I arranged the photos across the mantle. The stylish black and white Senior portrait of the twins, a photo of Aunt Gwen and myself that Ivy had taken at their Homecoming game, and the last picture that had been taken of my father, Arthur, and me.

I showed an old photo to the cat. "Here's my grandparents on their anniversary. Morgan and Rose. They called themselves Mo and Ro." Luna rubbed against the ornate frame, and I gave the cat's head a pat and placed the photo on the mantle. I set the picture of a toddler-aged me with my grandmother Rose in the gardens at the center of the display.

Luna jumped in the cardboard box and began to swat enthusiastically at the bubble wrap.

I left her to it, and added another photo; an informal shot of my brother and his family. Bran and Lexie sat on the porch swing of the manor. Lexie held the baby and Morgan who'd been named after his great-grandfather, sat grinning between his parents.

I unwrapped another frame. "Here's an old picture," I announced, in case my ghostly roommate was listening. "This is of you, Irene, with your brother, and your sister Faye." I placed the photo carefully with the others. There were a few other photos in the box, but I didn't unwrap them. I left them where they were, and tucked the box back in the bottom of the closet. "New house, new beginnings," I told myself.

I added a pair of mercury glass candle holders to the arrangement, dug through my stash of candles, popped a couple of pumpkin spice scented candles in the holders, and lit them. Luna decided to investigate under the couch, while I arranged the new pillows, and draped the throw across the end of the sectional. Finally I sat down and stretched my legs out.

I got back up made a few tiny adjustments to the photos on the mantle, and was congratulating myself on accomplishing yet another goal, when a knock on the front door had me spinning in surprise.

I went to the door, opened it and discovered Holly on the front porch.

She wasn't alone. Duncan Quinn stood with her.

CHAPTER THREE

"Autumn," Holly said. "I've asked Duncan to come over and see about completing your renovations."

Stunned, I could only stand there and stare. Duncan wore those same sexy jeans that were torn through at the knee, sneakers, and a navy t-shirt that stretched tight across his chest. I felt a little hitch of attraction in my belly and firmly ignored it.

Duncan nodded. "Holly tells me you've lost another contractor."

Mentally I yanked myself back to attention, and glared at my meddling cousin. "Oh she did, did she?"

"Yup," Holly said cheerfully, and with an innocent smile, she pushed past me into the living room.

Duncan stopped at the threshold. "Want to show me what you've got?" Duncan asked.

My eyes jumped to his. "I beg your pardon?"

"The bathroom," he said blandly. "I'd be happy to take a look, work up a bid on finishing it. But only if you're comfortable working with me."

Before I could say anything, the front door decided to swing open wider all on its own. I slanted my eyes to the door. Without warning, Duncan fell forward, straight into me and across the threshold. His chest slammed into mine, and we instinctually grabbed onto each other's arms for support as we staggered back.

"I'm so sorry," I said, steadying myself. *Oh god,* I thought as my fingers trailed over his biceps. *He felt wonderful.*

"Sorry," Duncan said as he straightened. "Something hit me hard, right in the back."

I badly wanted to test the strength of those biceps, and started to give in to the temptation. But I saw movement, and yanked Duncan out of the way right before the front door slammed shut on him.

"What the hell?" he said, while a soft female laugh drifted around us.

"Well that was subtle," I muttered to my ghostly roommate.

Duncan raised his eyebrows. "So it's true, the bungalow *is* haunted." He belatedly let go of me.

"By my great-aunt, Irene Bishop," I admitted. "She's the reason I've gone through so many contractors."

Holly stood in the living room, grinning at us. "Told you," she said to Duncan.

"I thought you were joking," he admitted.

I crossed my arms. "Unfortunately, no."

"Well as long as I'm here," Duncan began, "show me this bathroom that you need finished."

I tossed up my hands in defeat. "Fine." I stepped off the landing and into the living room.

"Is that going to be alright with you, Miss Bishop?" Duncan called out, staying where he was.

From across the room, the door to the bathroom slowly opened with a loud haunted house style creak.

"Oh for goddess' sake!" I rolled my eyes at Irene's theatrics, and marched towards the new bathroom.

Duncan chuckled, and stepped down to follow me. I tried not to laugh when he started whistling the theme from the old *Ghostbusters* movie.

An hour later, the two of us sat alone at the kitchen table while Duncan worked up a bid for the downstairs bathroom. Luna had gone off exploring the house, and Holly had made some lame excuse and had left us alone once Duncan began to survey the room. To my relief, my great-aunt's ghost was making herself scarce.

At least I hoped she was.

Duncan handed me the bid sheet and began to go down the points for the costs of tiling the floor and shower stall, mounting the fixtures, installing wainscoting, baseboards and painting. He'd been nothing but casually friendly and completely professional.

I'd managed to keep my mind off his body, and was finally starting to relax a little. His prices were fair, and maybe it was coincidence, but since I already had most of the supplies, he could start the work on Monday. He'd informed me that the reno would be complete in a couple of weeks, and that he would work on my bathroom in between his other jobs.

I sat back, trying to decide what to do. I truly wanted the bathroom finished, the possibility of that sorely tempted me. However, I really didn't like the idea of being manipulated into this situation by my witchy relatives—both the living and the dead.

Luna chose that moment to make her presence known by hopping into an empty chair. Her head popped up above the table. "*Meow*?"

"Who's this?" Duncan asked.

"This is Luna," I said, smiling as the cat reached out a paw and pulled a pencil off the table. It hit the floor and rolled. "I adopted her yesterday."

"Shelter cat?" Duncan asked, holding out his fingers for the cat to sniff.

"I found her in the gardens, and rescued her. The vet said she was healthy besides needing a little food and love, so I decided to take her in."

Luna rubbed the side of her face against Duncan's outstretched hand. "So I'll have supervision when I'm here," he said.

"Yeah, you will. Both the cat *and* the ghost. If you're up for that?"

"I can handle a ghost." Duncan smiled. "It'll be fine."

I studied the sheet in front of me. "Well, if you're sure—I'll go get my checkbook and give you the deposit."

"Okay," Duncan said, focusing on the cat who'd begun to purr.

I excused myself and went upstairs to the second bedroom I'd been using as an office. I congratulated myself at keeping any stray thoughts about him blocked, quickly wrote out a check, and jogged back down the stairs. "Here you go," I said, only to stop short as Luna was sitting in the middle of the kitchen table with her nose pressed up against Duncan's.

I handed Duncan the check and scooped up Luna. "She shouldn't be on the table."

Duncan pocketed the check and handed me a copy of the bid. "I'll be back Monday morning, before eight, to get started."

"That's fine." I set Luna on the floor. "I leave for the museum at eight thirty."

He stood and gathered up his things. "By the way, I really like how your kitchen turned out. You bumped out the old dining room wall to expand the kitchen, right?"

"That's right." I nodded. "Which also gave me room to add a bathroom on this level."

"Smart," Duncan said as he walked through the living room. "You've got some great colors in here. I like the rusty orange against the gray."

"Thanks," I said, following him to the front door. I tried my best not to act stiff or overly formal. *You're an adult,* I reminded myself. *And as such I was surely mature enough to handle the man working on my bathroom.* I congratulated myself on not checking him out as he walked in front of me. And I was so busy applauding my personal restraint that I tripped up the one stair to the landing and bumped into Duncan.

"Sorry." *So much for sophistication,* I thought.

"No worries." Duncan steadied me without any reaction. "See you Monday."

***

The following Monday he showed up right on time. I watched as he began to unload his truck. Making the mental effort to keep my thoughts and emotions protected from him, I paused and addressed my roommates. First: the ghostly one. "Okay Aunt Irene, he's here. So please, *please* play nice and let me get the renovations complete."

The cat was chomping away on her kibble, but lifted her head when I spoke to her. "Luna," I began, "be a good girl and don't get into any mischief while I'm gone."

The cat stared at me for a moment, then went back to her food and ignored me.

"Good morning." I held the back door open for Duncan as he carted in a couple of buckets of grout.

"Hello." Duncan took the buckets directly to the bathroom and returned a moment later. "I'll install the wainscoting today, then start the tile in the shower."

"One can only hope."

"It'll be fine," Duncan assured me. Then he spoke to the room. "Good morning, Miss Irene."

I raised an eyebrow. "You're taking the whole ghost thing remarkably well."

"Wouldn't be the first time I've run into a residual haunting on a job site."

"I'm not sure what type of haunting this would be classified as." I smiled blandly when the basement door opened all on its own.

"She only wants to make sure that we know she's still here." Duncan shrugged it off. "It'll be fine."

Luna scampered over, sat in front of him, and promptly swatted at Duncan's boot laces. To my surprise he bent down and scratched behind her ears. "Luna seems to like you," I said as the cat leaned against him. "I hope she won't bother you while you're working."

"I'm used to working around pets. It's fine," he said again. "Don't worry so much."

"This is for the back door." As I'd done with the other contractors, I handed him an extra key to the bungalow so he could let himself in and out as needed.

Duncan accepted the key. "Well, I'll get started. Have a good day."

I nodded and picked up my purse and lunch. "Call if you have any questions."

"Will do." Duncan went off towards the bathroom, and I headed towards the back door. Luna sat in a sunbeam on the kitchen floor and began to clean her paws.

"You girls, behave yourselves while I'm gone," I said softly to the cat *and* to my ghostly roommate.

Luna spared me a glance and went back to her grooming. The door to the basement shut with a soft click, so I let myself out the back door and headed to work.

I was distracted all day thinking of Duncan being in my house. I had to talk myself out of leaving at lunch to go and check on him. I reached for my cell phone a dozen times throughout the day, wanting to call and see how things were going. I hadn't done that with any of the other contractors, but I rationalized my behavior as concern—especially after three other contractors had been scared off the job.

By the time four thirty rolled around, my boss Dr. Meyer had left and I had completed proofing the invitations to a fundraiser for both the University library and the museum expansion. The event would be formal and hosted by the Drake family. The event was slated for the first Saturday in November. I'd actually enjoyed working on it, as the theme was a black and gold masquerade.

How I felt about going to the Drake mansion for the event was another thing altogether. I shook myself out of my thoughts, quickly straightened up my desk, shut everything down and locked up the office.

When I arrived back at the bungalow, Duncan's truck was gone. I let myself in the front door to the scent of lilacs perfuming the air, and Luna waiting for me on the little landing. "Hi kitty," I said, bending to pet her.

With Luna trailing along, I went directly to check on the progress in the bathroom. What I saw had me sighing happily. The wainscoting was in place. The design was in the classic craftsman style, and as I'd hoped, it helped make the new lower bathroom look as if it belonged in the home. The tile in the shower stall was underway. Little yellow spacers were between the white subway tiles, and they marched about half way up the shower stall.

"We might actually have a second working bathroom soon," I said to whoever was listening. In answer, the fragrance of lilacs grew stronger and then faded away. Luna leaned against my leg. "Come on, cat." I scooped her up. "Let's get some supper." I carried her into the kitchen, feeling more upbeat than I had in a long time.

Over the next few weeks the shower stall was tiled and grouted, and the lighting was installed. The new wainscoting had been painted bright white, and the walls were now a soft shell pink. The basket weave pattern floor tiles were in and grouted too, and the toilet was hooked up and operational. All that was left to do was the mounting of the chrome legged sink, hanging up the medicine cabinet, and installing the glass shower door. Which Duncan assured me he'd have finished very soon.

To my relief, Duncan and I had gotten along with no

difficulties or awkwardness of any kind as he came and went during the reno. We'd fallen into a sort of friendly routine, and fortunately Aunt Irene had been on her best behavior. At least I assumed she'd been, as Duncan hadn't mentioned any problems with the ghost the couple days a week that he was at the bungalow.

My birthday came and went with a small family celebration. I'd cleaned up there with a few gift cards to the local hardware super-store. Which got me to thinking about replacing the upstairs bathroom sink and faucet. Hopefully I could find something more 1920's Craftsman style appropriate. I considered asking Duncan about installing it for me, as I didn't want to tackle plumbing myself.

September rolled into October, and I studied that old cookbook of Irene's in the evenings. Her recipes were fascinating and their titles, hilarious. As Irene had adapted, amended and altered the recipes along with their names: *Lies Be Gone Lemon Bars, No Strings Spaghetti Sauce, Orgasm Ambrosia Salad, Turn Him from Sour to Sweet Coleslaw, Really Passionate Raspberry Lemonade*, and *Chocolate Sin Cake.*

I wasn't surprised to see astrological symbols doodled in the margins, and recommended lunar phases listed along with the baking times. After all, Irene had come from a family of Witches. Why wouldn't her cookbook have a magickal slant as well?

The museum staff was having a potluck luncheon on the first Friday of October, and I'd been tagged to bring a dessert. I read over the Lemon Bar recipe and thought that sounded like a winner. I worked up a batch and had to admit, they smelled divine.

Since I was on a roll, I scanned through the cookbook, found the raspberry lemonade recipe, and mixed up a pitcher full of that using the leftover lemons. I added some fresh raspberries, covered the pitcher with plastic wrap and left it in the fridge to chill and hopefully become pink overnight. I didn't have the dark raspberry liqueur the recipe called for, but I figured it would taste fine without it.

When the timer sounded on the oven, I took out the cake pan and allowed the dessert to cool on a rack on the counter. The following morning, I sprinkled the lemon bars with powdered sugar, snapped the lid on the pan and brought them to work.

I set the pan at the end of the table along with a few other desserts, propped the little card I'd made next to it that listed my name, what the dessert was, and that it was nut free. I hoped they'd be a hit.

I was late getting to lunch, and found myself as the last person in line. With a shrug, I helped myself to whatever was left over from the buffet. By the time I made it down to the end of the tables, my lemon bars were completely gone. There weren't even any crumbs left. *I guess they'd gone over really well.* I took an empty seat next to Julian Drake, who appeared to be finishing up a lemon bar.

"Hi Julian," I said as I sat down. "Do you like the

lemon bars?"

"I managed to get the last little piece." He smiled. "It was excellent." He wiped his fingers on a napkin.

"I'm surprised they're all gone," I admitted. "So what do you think—"

Julian cut me off. "I think that I like your hair much better since you let it grow back out."

"Wait, what?" I said, flabbergasted at the comment.

"I also think that you are an asset to the museum," Julian continued, ticking points off on his fingers. "I wished you worked in *my* department, and I hope someday we can become real friends."

Shocked at the admission, I promptly dropped my fork. It bounced off the table and landed on the floor. *Where in the sweet hell had all of that come from?* I goggled at Julian's casual declarations.

"Let me go get you another fork." Julian popped up, took his plate to the trash, picked up a new fork for me and cheerfully came back.

"I'm such a klutz," I muttered, and took the fork from him. "Thank you."

"You're welcome." He patted my shoulder in a brotherly way. "I don't think you're clumsy, by the way. I think you're too busy *seeing* everything else—and because of that, you don't always focus on what's right in front of you."

"Oh." I blinked at him.

"That's what I told Holly anyway," Julian said. "See you later." He strolled off and I sat there stupefied over our conversation.

"The lemon bars were wonderful!" A gray-haired secretary beamed over at me.

I focused on the middle aged woman. "Thanks Olivia, I'm so pleased that you enjoyed them. It's an old family recipe. One I hadn't tried before—"

"I had three," she interrupted and blushed. "I meant I had one—no three." Her face went red and her hand fluttered to her throat. She opened her mouth, shut it and shook her head. "I'm glad we did the potluck lunch today, it gave me a chance to get away from my boss."

"Oh?" *Oh,* I supposed was the safest thing to say. Then I wondered. "Who's your boss?"

"Jordan Maxwell. He's such a fussy, pompous ass."

I had to agree, the director of the historical society *was* a pain in the ass, but I was taken aback to hear her say that *out loud*. Before I could respond, Olivia stood suddenly and marched out of the lunch room.

I noticed that people were leaving the lunchroom in droves. Within moments I was sitting there alone. "How weird," I said, and ate my lunch alone.

I wandered back to my office and found Dr. Meyer sitting at his desk and speaking on the phone. He spotted me, and said a hasty goodbye to the caller. "Did you manage to get some lunch?" he asked.

"I did." I sat back at my desk and smiled over at him. "The lemon bars I made were all gone. I was looking forward to trying them. Did you eat one?"

"I'm not one for desserts." He tugged at his tie. "But

since you made them, I gave it a whirl."

"Don't leave me in suspense!" I chuckled. "Tell me the truth, did you—"

"I'm falling in love with your Great Aunt Faye," he blurted out, and flushed to his hairline.

"You're *what*?"

"I can't believe I said that." Dr. Meyer jumped up and began to pace.

Faye and Dr. Meyer—Hal, had been casually seeing each other since last year, when Ivy had tangled with that entity that had been haunting her dorm. I thought their friendship was good for the both of them, as they were both widowed. Plus Hal was fascinated by psychic phenomena and the paranormal, so the legacy of magick didn't faze him. But *this* tidbit of information had totally caught me off guard.

"I didn't know things had become so serious between you two," I said.

"Yes it's *serious*. We've been sleeping together for months." He stopped pacing and stared at me.

"You're sleeping together?" I managed to say, wondering who was more horrified at his confession—him or me.

"Yes, as in sex." Dr. Meyer rolled his eyes as if I was a little slow. "We have quite a lot of sex, actually."

"*Oh my god*," I squeaked. Now my face was turning red.

"Excuse me." Dr. Meyer escaped into his office, shutting the door firmly behind him.

I braced my elbows on my desk, dropped my head into my hands, and tried not to laugh. *It wasn't funny,* I told myself. *Not at all.* "Aw hell." I gave up. "Yes it is."

***

I came home that evening as Duncan was carting tools and supplies out of the bathroom.

"Guess what?" he said with a grin.

"What?"

"Your bathroom is done."

"Don't tease me," I said.

"Never," he replied, straight-faced.

"Really?" I dumped everything on the kitchen table.

"Yes, it's done."

I raced to see for myself and skidded to a stop in the doorway. "It's perfect," I breathed.

Duncan moved beside me as I admired the space. "I have to admit the pale pink on the walls above the white painted wainscoting actually looks good," he said. "At first, I thought the color would be too fussy."

I smirked at him. "What's the matter Quinn? Did the pink paint threaten your masculinity?"

"I'm trying to give you a compliment," he said dryly.

"Ooh, I'm all aflutter." I snarked, and wondered what he'd say if he ever saw the old cabinet that I'd repainted for bathroom storage.

"Anyway, the color works," he said.

"I can't wait to get the finishing touches in here." I

opened the glass shower door and admired the white subway tile and dark grout.

"I wiped it down," he said, "but you'll want to give it a good cleaning before you use it," Duncan advised.

I knelt down and trailed my fingertips over the floor. "The basket weave tile has exactly the vintage kind of vibe that I wanted." I jumped up and went to try the sink.

"Where did you find the chrome legged pedestal sink?" Duncan asked while I turned on the water at the new faucets.

"Aunt Faye helped me track one down online. It came from a salvage company that restores old pieces."

"Would you mind passing that company's information along to me?" Duncan asked. "It would come in handy for other rehabs in the future."

"Sure." I beamed over at him. "Duncan, this is wonderful. Thank you so much for taking on the project."

"You're welcome," he said. "I'll go haul out the last of my things and give you the final invoice."

"Okay," I answered, opening the medicine cabinet, and sighing over the bathroom. All I had to do was clean it, bring in the linen cabinet, hang up my art and put out the towels. Then it would be ready to go!

I forced myself to stop mooning over the bathroom and went into the kitchen. I could see Duncan through the back door, loading up his truck and decided that such a momentous occasion as having completed renovations called for a celebration. I took the lemonade out of the fridge, added some ice cubes to two tumblers and poured us each a glass.

He let himself in the back door, and I handed him the pink lemonade. "Here you go."

"Same color as your bathroom," he said and took a sip.

I sampled it. "The lemonade is a family recipe, I thought I'd try it out. It originally called for raspberry liqueur, but I think it's okay as is."

"Yeah, it's really good," Duncan agreed.

I tapped my glass to his. "I'm really glad that we're friends again, Duncan."

"Friends?" he said, as if trying out the word.

"Well, yeah," I said. "Why can't we be friends?"

Duncan drained his glass and set the empty tumbler on the counter. Silently, he held out the invoice.

I automatically reached for the paper, and our fingers brushed. Only the barest of touches, and I felt a jolt of power go all the way to my toes. My gaze snapped to his, and those bright blue eyes locked on mine.

"*That's* why we can't just be friends," he said softly.

We stood perfectly still, staring at each other. Since Irene had shoved him through the door a few weeks before, we hadn't physically touched each other again. In fact we'd both been vigilant to avoid any sort of physical contact at all.

The blood pounded in my ears and I forced myself to exhale. I hadn't felt that jolt of power in years, almost three to be exact. Now that our personal magicks had gotten a sampling of each other again, I felt my stomach tighten. With effort, I pulled back on my energy that had started to reach out for his. It wasn't easy, and I trembled.

"You're stronger than you used to be." Duncan's voice was soft and considering.

I placed the invoice on the counter. Deliberately, I unclenched my fingers from around the glass I held and set it on the kitchen table before I broke it. "I had to learn personal restraint the hard way."

"Meaning what?" He wanted to know.

I could have kicked myself for admitting that to him. "Never mind." I cleared my throat. "I was going to offer to cook you a friendly dinner to say thanks for all the hard work you put in. But if you don't think we can be friends..."

"I didn't mean it like that." Duncan stepped slightly closer.

It took everything I had to stay where I was. "What *did* you mean?"

He blew out a breath. "Dinner would be great."

"Tomorrow night work for you?" I heard myself ask.

"Sure." Duncan smiled down into my eyes. "Want me to bring some wine?"

I stepped back. "This isn't a date, Quinn."

"I meant that in a *friendly* way," he said. "I bet Violet brought wine when she came over and brought you that house plant."

Ellen Dugan

"How'd you know that?" I frowned.

He tipped his head towards the cyclamen on the counter. "Her magickal energies are all over that blooming plant. Also the house had a 'Girls Night' vibe on it the first time I came over."

"Girls night?" I rolled my eyes. "Yeah, we were wild women."

"Like pillow fights in your underwear, wild?"

"Absolutely," I shot back. "All in movie style slow motion too."

Duncan tossed back his head and laughed. It hit me like a ton of bricks how much I'd missed that sound. I tried to yank the conversation back on track. "Six o'clock, Quinn. If you want a friendly dinner, be here."

"Sounds good," he said cheerfully.

I opened the back door. "Fine. I'll see you tomorrow."

"Good night." He nodded and went out the door, down the porch and across the back yard.

As he walked away, I was so busy admiring the way his jeans fit him that it took me a moment to realize that I was staring at him. Again. I caught myself, flushed a little and closed the door, wondering what I had gotten myself into.

That night I busted out Irene's cookbook and got to work. The *Chocolate Sin Cake* recipe had come out beautifully. I tucked the two decadent layers of chocolate cake and tart cherry filling topped with dark chocolate frosting in the fridge. The recipe had called

60

for pitting the cherries by hand, and actually included a little poem to the goddess Venus. I'd been so happy and excited about the reno being complete that I'd gone all in. I'd cranked up some music, sipped a glass of wine and had a blast making Irene's campy cake recipe under the light of the full moon.

Saturday morning I got up early, snipped some oregano and parsley from the garden and diced up the last of the Roma tomatoes that I'd grown. I gave the *No Strings Spaghetti Sauce* a try, and put the sauce on low in the crock pot and left it to simmer. That way all I would have to do later was boil the pasta, add the sauce, and toss a bagged salad.

I scrubbed the kitchen down, then tackled removing the construction dust out of the bathroom and hung up my framed antique prints. I dragooned Bran into helping me haul the small cabinet in from the garage that I'd painted in a pink color a few shades deeper than the walls. I placed a trio of glass apothecary jars inside, stacked bath towels in white and pink, added toilet paper, hair products and a hair dryer, too.

"Renovations complete!" I said, flipping a fuzzy pink rug down in front of the shower. I draped the hand towels over the rack by the sink and indulged in a celebratory booty shake.

By five forty-five, I'd changed into a simple maxi dress in mossy green. I tied an apron over my outfit to protect it and put the pasta on to boil. The salad was in a bowl, and I set the kitchen table while Luna perched on Morgan's stepstool and kept a watchful eye on my dinner preparations.

Duncan showed up a few minutes before six. He looked wonderful in dark jeans and a soft khaki button down shirt. He smiled at me and my heart gave one hard *thud* in reaction.

I took a bracing breath and opened the door. "Hello Duncan."

CHAPTER FOUR

I served the salad and pasta, and we settled into an easy conversation about his work and my job at the museum. Luna played chaperone, sitting in an empty chair at the table and watching us. It was casual, relaxed, and as far as I could tell, without a hint of romance.

Duncan helped me load up the dishwasher after dinner, and then I took the cake out of the fridge. I gingerly set the glass cake plate on the table and lifted the dome that covered it. I let out a quiet sigh of relief that I'd managed to get it to the table without a disaster.

"Wow." Duncan whistled between his teeth. "You made that?"

"I did," I said, picking up the cake knife. "It's called *Chocolate Sin.*"

I cut a few slices and laid them on the plates as carefully as if they were dynamite. Somehow I managed to serve the dessert with no mishaps.

Duncan tried a bite, and closed his eyes. "Mmmm."

His voice was low and throaty, and it hit me as sort of sexual.

I restrained myself from pumping my fist in the air, and instead took a bite of the cake. The dark chocolate seemed to explode in my mouth. The cherry filling was the right balance of tart to the sweet frosting. I let out a happy sigh. "That's a winner, Aunt Irene."

The sun set and filled the kitchen with a rosy sort of light. The air went heavy and it was like we were the only two people on earth. Part of me was aware of the shift in the atmosphere and another part of me settled into it and enjoyed the relaxed and indulgent vibe.

Duncan took another bite. "This was a recipe of Irene's?"

I pointed at the red book that I had displayed on a stand on the counter. "I found an old cookbook of Irene's when I moved in. The recipes so far have all come out really well. I made lemon bars for work, and folks devoured them."

Duncan cleaned his plate, and gazed longingly at the cake. Without a word, I cut another, larger slice. "Thanks," he said and dove right in.

I talked myself out of a second serving and watched, fixated as Duncan swiped his fork through the cherry filling of his slice. He lifted the fork to his mouth and slowly sucked the cherries off the tines.

The gesture hit me in the gut, and I swallowed past a lump in my throat. He wasn't even paying attention to me. He was totally absorbed in the taste and textures of the dessert. And somehow that was sexy as hell. *Get a grip, Autumn,* I thought even as I fumbled my plate.

Duncan glanced down at my hands. "You have frosting on your fingers," he said, lifting my hand. To my shock, he began to sample the smeared frosting.

My heart slammed into my ribs. "So, you like the cake?" My voice sound all breathy to my own ears, and I wondered what was happening.

"Yes, I like it," he said in a low voice.

A thought flashed crazily through my mind: *I'd like to smear that chocolate icing all over him and lick it off. Slowly.* I remembered a moment too late that we were sitting close to each other, and if my thoughts were strong or loud enough, he would 'hear' them.

His eyes snapped to mine. "Honey, I'd be happy to return the favor." His voice was husky, and had me struggling not to squirm in my chair.

Oh shit.

He was sitting very still, and watching me. Not unlike a predator waiting for its prey to make one wrong move—before it pounced.

I couldn't seem to help myself. I moved.

With a primal sort of growl, Duncan was out of his chair and hauling me into his arms quicker than I could blink.

"I—" was the only thing I managed to vocalize before his mouth swooped down. All I could taste was the cherries and the dark chocolate as his tongue swept over mine. The magick that we'd once shared with no thought of the consequences burst free and wound around the two of us.

I reached up and grabbed ahold of his hair and pulled him closer. He began to trail kisses down my throat, and my head fell back as his hands passed over me...

Then everything changed.

I flinched as something foreign shoved me aside. I struggled against the invasion, even as I felt my lips curl up. "That recipe never disappoints," I heard a different female voice say.

Duncan froze.

I felt my head tip down to meet his eyes. Like I was no longer driving the bus, but only along for the ride. *Release me!* I thought furiously at the unfamiliar energy that had swept in and claimed my body for its own.

Soon... The voice whispered through my mind.

My heart beat loudly in my chest, while I gazed at Duncan through a new set of eyes.

"Autumn?" Duncan whispered.

"No," I heard the other say. "No, not Autumn. Irene."

Get out, Irene! I thought. *I'll be damned if you're going to use me like a puppet!* I began to shake from the effort of fighting her possession. *Get out!* I screamed silently.

Duncan tightened his grip on my arms. "Release her. Right the fuck now!" he growled. Luna agreed with the sentiments. She let out a loud wail in the background.

"You have to help me," I heard Irene say. "Help me bring back what was secreted away."

"I won't help you do anything!" Duncan gave my/her shoulders a brisk shake.

I laughed in a voice that wasn't mine. "I'd never hurt her, I only wanted to get your attention."

"You have it," Duncan said through his teeth. "Now go, or I'll banish you from here and make sure that your spirit never finds any peace—not *ever*."

"Temper, temper," she said.

I'd been listening and waiting for my chance, simultaneously raising as much personal power as I could, until I vibrated with it. When Duncan had threatened her, Irene's grip on me had lessened. *Now. Now was my chance,* I realized, and tapped into Duncan's magickal energy, using it to bolster my own.

"Get out!" I shouted, pushing against her with everything I had. Mine and Duncan's combined magick blasted out, and I felt that foreign presence slide away.

My knees buckled, and she was gone.

I found myself half-sitting on the kitchen floor a bit later, while Duncan rocked me in his arms.

"Autumn?" he called my name softly.

"Yeah?" I struggled to sit up.

"Look at me." Duncan framed my face with his hands. He searched my eyes and I watched his shoulders drop in relief. "It's you. You're back."

I wrapped my hands around his wrists and held on. "I'm okay."

Duncan dropped his forehead against mine. "I don't think I like this relative of yours."

"I'm liking her less and less myself."

We stayed sitting together on the floor that way for a while, taking comfort from each other. Luna strolled over and climbed up Duncan's legs and walked over to paw at my chest.

"Hi kitty," I said as the cat leaned her head in and began to purr.

"Come on," Duncan nudged the cat aside, rose to his feet and pulled me up with him.

I wobbled, and he wrapped an arm around my waist. "The couch." I pointed and he led me to it. We'd barely sat down before Luna jumped up and settled into my lap. I ran my hand over her head and felt comforted by her purrs and Duncan's arm around my shoulders.

"Has this ever happened to you before?" Duncan asked.

"You mean the possession?" I said, wanting to be clear.

"Has it?"

"No, it hasn't."

"Are you losing blocks of time?" Duncan wanted to know.

I shuddered. "No, I haven't been."

"You need to be careful Autumn," Duncan said. "With you being a sensitive, you're already open to the spirit realm."

"Well I don't want to be *that* open ever again!"

"Here, take this." Duncan reached up and unclasped a chain from around his neck.

The pendant was a large, dark, oval shaped stone. As he held it out to me, it caught the light and suddenly began to shimmer in an amazing peacock blue and gold against the black. "What type of stone is this?" I asked.

"Labradorite. It's a stone that deflects unwanted energies, *and* it's highly protective."

I held it in my palm for a moment, sensing the vibrations that came from the pendant. The chain was long enough that I was able to slip it over my head. "It's lovely, thank you." As soon as it rested against my chest, I felt a sense of calm. We sat silently together for a while, and it was comforting for the both of us.

"Would you like me to call someone?" Duncan offered.

"No," I said, leaning closer to him. "I'm very glad you were here tonight."

"So am I." Duncan gave my shoulders a squeeze. "Sort of like old times, eh?" Duncan said half joking.

His bright blue eyes were so close to mine, and the longing I felt for him had me trembling. I licked my lips against a suddenly dry mouth. "Duncan, I—"

Before I could finish, he pressed his lips to mine and shared energy with me. His mouth stayed closed, but power crackled through my body, arching my back and pushing my chest further against his. My heart pounded, my ears buzzed, and all my muscles throbbed at the blending of my energies and his.

I kissed him back every bit as hard, and somewhere in the back of my mind I had the presence of mind to stop before things got too far out of hand.

We pulled apart at the same second. Both of us gasping for breath and at the combination of magick, attraction and desire. I felt much steadier from his contribution, but still I unwound myself from him and eased back. "Thanks," I said quietly. "I feel stronger."

"Any time," he said.

Who was I trying to fool pretending that we could only be friends? I wondered. *There would always be this connection between us.*

"So," Duncan said, cutting off my inner ramblings. "I think we need to be really truthful with each other. All things considered."

"Agreed." I shifted on the couch and tried to get my rampaging hormones under control.

Duncan leaned his head back against the sofa. "Since we're being honest, I'm going to admit that I want you," he said raggedly. "Very badly."

My breath caught in my throat, while a few sexy possibilities raced through my mind. It took everything I had to sit still and to try and remain calm. "And in that spirit of honesty, I will admit that I want you too," I said. "Though, I'm not sure that this feeling is completely natural."

Duncan recoiled. "What?"

"She said, *That recipe never disappoints*," I reminded him.

Duncan leaned back. "That's right. You did mention earlier that the chocolate cake was Irene's recipe."

I nodded. "From what I could tell, Irene had adapted the original recipe in that cookbook, and she renamed it *Chocolate Sin*." I studied the decadent chocolate dessert that still sat on the cake stand in the kitchen. "I think we may both be under a sort of magickal influence."

"Oh boy." Duncan's eyes grew large.

"Makes me wonder if that recipe was actually a sort of culinary spell."

"A love spell?"

I thought about our reactions to the dessert. "Passion inducing spell, maybe."

Without a word we both shifted to opposite ends of the couch and were no longer touching. Luna moved between the two of us. She glared at me, shifted to consider Duncan and sat down in the center of the sofa like a kitty chaperone.

"I'm very sorry," I began.

"Stop." Duncan held up a hand. "I know you'd never purposefully unleash something like that. Would your Aunt Faye know more about this type of magick?"

"According to what Aunt Faye told me, the family wasn't happy with the way Irene practiced her Craft, back in the day."

Duncan frowned. "Meaning what, exactly?"

"That's just it," I said. "I don't know." I patted Luna's back for comfort. "I haven't been able to find much out about the woman, besides the fact that she liked lilacs."

"I thought I smelled them when I was here working the other day," Duncan said. "But they only bloom in the spring, right?"

"That's correct," I said. "There are a few really old, leggy lilac shrubs in the back by the garage. I pruned them back hard this spring hoping to encourage more blooms out of them next year..." I trailed off.

"How old are the shrubs?" Duncan asked.

"I'd estimate them to be at least fifty years old. They were in bad shape."

"So it's possible that Irene planted them herself?"

"There's no way to know for sure, but my instincts say that she did."

"Do you have any other information on the woman that might be helpful?"

"Actually yes. It was Irene who added to the wrought iron fence that surrounds the estate. She divided her yard from the manor's. Closing in the bungalow and separating the yards."

"And separating herself from the family, too." Duncan said.

I took off my glasses and pressed my fingers to the bridge of my nose. "Aunt Faye told us that her sister was a 'difficult woman', and because of that I haven't mentioned to Aunt Faye my interactions with the ghost, or the little cookbook that we found." I tried not to cringe at the disapproving vibes radiating off Duncan. "I didn't want to upset Faye," I tried to explain.

"When did you find the cookbook?"

"That first day," I said, putting my glasses back on. "When we began to clean and paint the bungalow. Holly found the book. It had been hidden behind a loose panel in the pantry."

"So it may have been stashed there all the time the Greenes owned the home?"

"That's what Holly and I figured." I shrugged. "I thought it was kitschy and cool, you know? A vintage recipe book belonging to an ancestor, so I displayed it on a stand in the kitchen."

Duncan gave my shoulder a squeeze. "You couldn't have known."

"What do I do with it now?" I wondered.

"I'll admit I know next to nothing about kitchen magick," Duncan said. "But I think you'd better be very, very cautious before trying any of her other recipes."

"Agreed."

"You don't know any Kitchen Witches, do you?" Duncan said. "Maybe they could offer some advice."

"You know what?" A thought suddenly occurred to me. "I think I *do* know someone who can help. Let me make a quick call."

Candice Jacobs showed up fifteen minutes later. She bounced into the house all good cheer, her platinum hair twisted up behind her head and secured with a hot pink clip. She wore denim shorts that had seen better days and a white t-shirt that read, *I'm a Pastry Chef I create magick. What's your superpower?*

"Thanks for coming over so quickly," I said, bending to give her a hug.

"Of course." She kicked her magenta flip flops off beside the door and stepped down into the living room. "Let's see this family cookbook of yours."

I introduced her to Duncan and they shook hands. Candice held onto his hand and tugged him down closer to her. "That's interesting," she said, studying his eyes.

I was surprised to see the petite Witch go nose to nose with Duncan. She might have been a foot shorter, but she more than held her own. "What's interesting?" I asked.

"Autumn, come over here." She held her free hand out.

I took her hand. She stood between the two of us and shifted her eyes from Duncan and finally to me. "Hate to break it to you kids, but you both have been nailed by a passion spell."

"We figured," Duncan said.

Candice dropped our hands and shook hers out. She walked into the kitchen and stopped in front of the table. "Hmmm." She narrowed her eyes at the cake on the stand and bent over to sniff at the dessert. "So is this our suspect?"

"It is." Duncan crossed his arms over his chest.

"Do you want to taste the cake?" I asked, thinking to get her a fork.

"Ah, no thanks," Candice said, her eyes dancing.

"I'm not really into threesomes these days."

While Duncan gaped at her, I started to laugh. "Oh my god, Candice, I didn't mean it like that!"

"I think maybe I should go," Duncan said.

"Oh," I said, surprised. "You don't have to."

"I'll call and check on you later." Duncan walked over to me and trailed a finger down my cheek. "Thanks for dinner. It was memorable." He nodded at Candice. "Nice to meet you."

Candice inclined her head. "See you around," she said.

Duncan went to the back door. "Keep the pendant on," he reminded me.

"I will," I promised.

He flashed a grin over his shoulder, and let himself out.

"Well," I said, more than a little surprised at his sudden exit.

"I guess he got spooked by my joke about a threesome." Candice shrugged.

"I've had a chance to get used to your humor. He hasn't." I went to the counter and lifted the old cookbook out of the stand. "Let's take this into the living room."

We made ourselves comfortable on the couch, and I handed the cookbook over to Candice. I waited and watched as she read through the recipe. "What do you think?" I asked when I couldn't take the suspense any longer.

"I think it's a freaking miracle that you somehow managed *not* to tear each other's clothes off and do it on the kitchen floor," she said, straight faced.

My eyes went wide. "Oh shit."

"Honey, how many years have you been practicing?" Candice asked.

"Around four," I said.

"My dad told me that you've had to learn pretty quickly, but Autumn, there's really no excuse for not seeing this recipe for the manipulative spell that it is."

Shocked at her harsh tone, I stammered. "Well, I—"

"Seriously girl, how could you *not* know?" Candice frowned. "For example, the symbols on the page!"

"The old astrological doodles?" I said. "I figured they were simply a decorative touch..." I trailed off as she glowered.

"I assume you did the recommended invocation to the goddess Venus?"

"The poem that was with the recipe? Yeah sure, I read it last night," I said, not following her.

"Out loud?" Candice asked.

Confused, by the question, I frowned. "Yes, out loud. Why does that matter?"

"You read this out loud last night? On a Friday, under the full moon?"

I adjusted my glasses. "Is that significant?"

"You dumbass!" Candice slammed a finger on the page. "This isn't a poem, it's an *invocation*."

"A what?"

"An invocation is basically an invitation to a deity to assist you," Candice said through her teeth. "*Or* it can be a request for them to come inside of you, allowing the supplicant to take on some of their attributes."

"Come inside of you?" I said.

"Yes, as in divine *possession*."

"Sweet baby Jesus," I said, borrowing one of my mother's favorite phrases. Now I was *scared.* I tried to breathe my way past the anxiety that gripped me.

"I can tell by the expression on your face that you honestly had no idea," Candice said softly.

"It's more than that," I admitted. "I once accidentally stepped in a *veve* and invoked Papa Legba."

"You overachiever, you."

I winced at her words. "Your father once said the exact same thing to me."

Candice patted my shoulder. "Okay, girlfriend, let's start simple." Her tone was gentler now. "You know your daily planetary correspondences, right?"

"The planets and magicks assigned to each day of the week? Yes I do."

Candice nodded. "Good. Tell me what the magickal correspondences are for a Friday."

I closed my eyes, recalled my early Craft lessons and began reciting. "Friday was named after the goddess Freya—Friday is Freya's day," I began. "Planetary correspondence is Venus, associated colors are pink and green, the metal is copper. Coordinating herbs would be violets, roses, spearmint and the willow tree."

"Correct," Candice said. "It also might interest you to know that some of the foods that are associated with Venus include; cherries, sugar, and vanilla."

"What about chocolate?" I asked, viewing the cake with new eyes.

"Chocolate is aligned to the planet Mars," Candice said. "And if you know your mythology, the god Mars was—"

"The lover of the goddess Venus," I finished for her.

"One of them anyway," Candice said. "So, taking all of this information into consideration, if you created a culinary spell using chocolate, cherries, vanilla and sugar, and invoked the goddess of sexual love on a Friday under a full moon..."

"Then I would've conjured up a spell to encourage passion and promote sex." I swallowed hard. I thought back to the night before. "Candice, when I baked that cake, I had some wine, danced around the kitchen, and sang along with the radio."

"In other words you raised a lot of energy. And all of it went into the spell."

Horrified, I jumped up and grabbed that cake stand off the table. I marched straight to the kitchen garbage can and dumped the cake. I yanked the water on in the sink, added detergent, and got the bubbles going. I stuck the glass stand in, went for the forks and dessert plates and began washing those by hand too.

Candice joined me at the sink. "Where do you keep your kitchen towels?" she asked easily. I pointed out the correct drawer and Candice quietly dried the dishes as I washed them. "It's going to be okay." Candice gave me a little hip bump.

"I'm more than a little upset that I unknowingly worked that sort of sexually manipulative spell. On Duncan Quinn of all people," I admitted.

Candice took the dishcloth from me and went over to the kitchen table. Competently, she wiped it down and drew a banishing pentagram in the air over the table. "Well, you learned a valuable lesson tonight, didn't you?"

I wiped my hands on a dry towel. "Yes, I did."

"I need to know," Candice said, walking back to the sink. "Have you worked up any other recipes from that cookbook?"

My stomach rolled over. "Only a couple."

"Show me." Candice draped the dishcloth over the faucet.

I fetched the cookbook and carried it to the table. Candice joined me as I sat and flipped through the pages searching for the lemon bar recipe. Looking at the recipe with new eyes I began to put it all together. "I worked this on a Thursday night. I also let it sit on the counter to cool, under the light of the waxing moon." I gulped.

"Where are they now?" Candice asked.

"I took the lemon bars to work and served them at the potluck."

"So those lemon bars got a double whammy of lunar

energy." Candice pursed her lips as she read over the recipe for *Lies Be Gone Lemon Bars*.

"Double whammy?" I asked.

"Lemons are a lunar fruit," she explained. "Did anything weird happen when folks ate the lemon bars?"

I dropped my head in my hands. "Yes, three people who'd eaten them spontaneously told me things I really didn't want to know."

Candice shook her head. "According to the recipe, to activate the magick, you have to ask the victim to tell you the truth, and then they can not lie to you."

"Victim?" I lifted my head. "That doesn't sound very nice."

Candice raised her eyebrows. "What part of 'manipulative magick' did you not understand?"

I dropped my head in my hands again as I thought back to Friday. "I asked them to tell me what they thought of the recipe. But now that I think about it, I never got to finish my sentence. I'm pretty sure all I was able to say was something like, *tell me what you think*."

"Learned more than you wanted, eh?" Candice sat back in her chair. "Were there any other recipes that you worked from this cookbook?"

I jerked up straight in my chair. "Oh no. I used the *No Strings Spaghetti Sauce* for supper tonight, and I did use the leftover lemons for the *Really Passionate Raspberry Lemonade*."

"By the old gods, woman," Candice swore, and

began to thumb through the cookbook searching for the recipes. She found them and began to read. "Is the spaghetti all gone?"

"Yes, we ate it all." I gulped nervously.

"Tomatoes are also aligned to the goddess Venus." Candice said.

I thought about the astrological correspondences, and took the book back to study the recipe for myself. "I made the sauce this morning, on a Saturday, during a waning moon. The book says for best results to work it on a Friday under the waxing moon."

"So the effects weren't quite as potent." Candice nodded.

I stared at the family cookbook with a growing sense of horror.

Candice raised her eyebrows. "The lemonade you made. Did the potion sit under the light of the moon?"

"Potion?" I hurriedly flipped to the page with the lemonade recipe.

"That's basically what this is." Candice pointed at the offending page.

"No." I shook my head. "I put it directly in the fridge to cool, and I didn't use the raspberry liqueur that it called for."

"Did you serve it tonight?"

"No, I didn't." I shut the cookbook and set it aside. "I did pour him a glass the other day..."

Candice rubbed her forehead. "Did anything weird happen?"

"I don't think so."

"Well you can thank your lucky stars for that."

"That raspberry lemonade is still in the fridge." I jumped to my feet.

"Let me see it, before you dump it." Candice stood and walked to the fridge. She pulled the pitcher out, sat the pitcher in the center of the table, and peeled back the plastic wrap. As before, she sniffed it cautiously. To my surprise she asked for a paper grocery bag, which I gave her, and then she motioned me to follow her outside.

We strolled out in the backyard. The waning moon was still rising as Candice stopped on the little brick path that led to my detached garage.

"What are you doing?" I asked.

"Watch," she said and poured out the lemonade on the bricks.

The liquid seemed to defy gravity as it slowly poured out of the pitcher. It shimmered under the light of the moon, and finally after an impossible moment, the lemonade landed on the bricks.

The lemonade coalesced, and took on a life of its own as the puddle reformed into the shape of a waning crescent moon. "That can't be good," I said.

"Your family crest is a waxing crescent moon, isn't it?" Candice asked.

"It is."

"Well, it's my opinion that the person who created this spell corrupted the magick, flipped it to a darker, but mirror image of what it was originally intended for."

"What do I do now?" I asked, horrified.

"Tonight, I'm going to clean it up for you." She stared at me hard. "Only this once, Autumn."

"I understand," I said, meeting her dark eyes.

Candice held her hand over the moon shaped puddle. "Magick be gone, spin round and about," she began. "Widdershins you shall turn, taking all that is baneful out."

The liquid began to spin in a counterclockwise motion, and Candice flipped her hand over, palm up and slowly bunched her fingers into a fist. "Disperse, be gone and fade away; this manipulative magick is no longer in play." She tossed her hand high and the liquid leapt off the bricks. It dissipated into the air, and was gone.

"Whoa," I said, thoroughly impressed.

"Where's your garbage can?" Candice asked.

"Along the side of the garage." I pointed to the big blue can.

"Be right back," she said, scooping up the paper bag and glass pitcher, she marched towards the can.

Curious as to what she was about, I followed her.

Candice placed the glass pitcher into the paper bag. She folded up the top, and to my surprise, the blonde threw the bag into the bottom of the can hard enough that the glass pitcher shattered inside of the bag. "The spell is forever broken, this magick is sealed by the words I have spoken." She let the hinged lid drop smartly, brushed off her hands and started back towards me.

"Though she is little, she is fierce!" I said, going for the Shakespeare quote.

Candice sketched a bow. "I could really go for a glass of wine."

"I think that could be arranged," I said. "So long as you promise to teach me how you did that."

"You want lessons?" Candice asked. "As in formal Craft training?"

I glanced over my shoulder to the spot where she'd banished the lemonade potion. "I think some kitchen witchery lessons might be a damn good idea, all things considered."

"I would be happy to work with you," Candice said, looping her arm through mine. "I bet I can whip you into shape."

"Whip?" I raised an eyebrow at her, not sure that she wasn't going for the double entendre.

"It's a baker's term." Candice winked. "Trust me."

CHAPTER FIVE

After Candice left I discovered that the family cookbook was open to a page I hadn't read yet. "I know I shut that book." I approached it warily and saw the recipe it was open to was entitled: *Applesauce Apologies*. "No way," I said in case my relative was floating around and listening. "Aunt Irene, this might be your way of saying that you're sorry. But it's not funny." I picked up the book and slid it back inside a kitchen cabinet.

I went to bed and was awake all night thinking over what had happened. Luna slept at the foot of the bed, and I watched as the moon worked its way across the sky.

Getting all stirred up by those culinary spells, *and* by Duncan, had left me feeling achy, needy, and sexually frustrated. I'd held back on a lot over the years. Especially after being with Rene, and having to be so careful with my personal energies. Clearly a part of me was tired of being tucked away in a box and ignored.

Dozens of sexy scenarios played through my mind of what *could* have happened. The two of us going at it on the kitchen table...me sitting on the counter and him standing between my thighs. Or us lying on the plush gray rug in front of the fireplace hearth, wrapped around each other, as Duncan brushed the hair back from my face...

Good grief, I thought, and tried to yank my imagination back under control. But it bounced right back with a vengeance. The scene of the two of us together on the rug suddenly morphed into a vision of the future...

Jack-o'-lanterns flickered on the hearth, and an orange light shone through the bungalow's front window. Duncan stared down into my eyes while he made love to me. I could feel the plush carpet on my back, and the warmth of his chest against mine. He caught my hands and stretched my arms up and over my head, holding me gently in place. "I love you," he said, and then our kiss went on forever.

I scrubbed my hands over my face. "What the hell?" I wondered. But the more I thought about the vision, the more turned on I got. I'd never had a sex vision before, and I wasn't sure how to react to what I'd *seen*. Jack-o'-lanterns on the hearth? It had to be Halloween. This approaching Halloween.

My mind raced back and forth questioning whether or not that had been a vision, or merely wishful thinking. Eventually I growled and tossed a decorative pillow across the room. It did make me feel mildly better at the thump it made when it bounced off the wall.

Somehow, I managed to talk myself out of calling Duncan to come over. I really wanted to think that I hadn't slipped so far under the influence of Irene's shady magick that I'd give into it by indulging in a late night booty call.

But damn it, I really wanted to.

Eventually, I'd fallen asleep for an hour and I'd dreamt not of more crazy and wild sex with Duncan, but instead of a parade of women all coming silently to the back door of the bungalow. One by one they'd lined up. Old and young, pretty and plain. Scratching on the glass of the windows, or tapping on the screen door. All of them with beseeching expressions on their faces. Each of the women holding out their hands, as if pleading for something.

I sat straight up in bed and shook my head clear of the dream. I sighed, still feeling as churned up as I had when I'd tried to sleep. The sun was up, the birds were singing and it was a pretty Saturday morning—and I had work to do. So, I rolled out of bed, put on my grubbiest clothes, and channeled all of that sexual frustration into yard work.

I mowed the grass, watered and weeded the flower beds, and cleaned the house from top to bottom. Which helped burn off the lingering effects of the passion spell, *and* it helped to settle me down somewhat.

Afterwards, I scrubbed up in the shower, made sure I ate a good lunch, and felt more clear headed, more like myself.

Later that afternoon I headed over to the Jacobs' home to meet up with Candice. It was a pretty day for a walk so I laced up my coral cross trainers, slipped on some khaki shorts and a creamy peasant style blouse, and took a leisurely walk. The Jacobs' house was a ranch style home, one of several where the older Victorian era homes ended and the more modern ones began.

I grinned at the scarecrow holding court in their front flower bed, flanked by hay bales and several pumpkins. The neatly manicured lawn was a bright green, and tidy window boxes were arranged along the front of the house.

As I rang the doorbell I noticed a coordinating pot of ivy and pansies by the front door. These matched the window boxes and appeared freshly planted. I nodded in approval at the orange and blue flowers all mixed cheerfully together. A golden trio of unplanted mums rested in their pots in the shade, alongside a garden trowel and a bag of daffodil bulbs. A smear of potting mix trailed across the porch.

Mrs. Jacobs ushered me straight back to her large kitchen. It was clear where Candice had gotten her looks. Her mother was also petite, with the same chocolate brown eyes and platinum hair that was turning beautifully to silver.

"Candice will be home in a little bit," she announced. "She got hung up at the new shop dealing with a plumbing issue."

"Well, I appreciate you letting me interrupt your afternoon, Mrs. Jacobs," I said.

"Nonsense," she said, setting a plate of sugar cookies before me. "Those chrysanthemums aren't going anywhere. And you can call me Carol."

"Thanks, Carol." I accepted a mug of tea from her.

Carol sat down across from me. "Candice told us about the cookbook you found, and the trouble it caused."

I tugged self-consciously on my peasant style shirt. "Well, I have to admit, I never figured that an old cookbook would be a potentially dangerous item."

"Considering the chaos the Blood Moon Grimoire caused a few years ago, I'm a little surprised you were so casual about having a book of unknown origin in your home to begin with." Her tone was light, but the warning was stern nonetheless.

"Good point." I sampled the cookie. "I suppose it was my curiosity that got the better of me. I know so little of Irene. Aunt Faye won't speak of her, and there is very little in the family history written about her."

"I knew your great aunt Irene," Carol admitted.

"You did?" I asked, surprised.

"Yes, I did."

I began to slide the labradorite pendant Duncan had given me back and forth on its chain. "Tell me."

"When I was a teenager, my friends used to dare each other to go to her back porch and pay for spells. Or love potions."

To her back door... The hair rose on the back of my neck. I recalled the dreams I'd had about the women all lined up at the back door of the bungalow. Holding out their hands as if begging...

I tried to keep my tone light. "Did you ever go to Irene's?"

"Yes, I did," Carol said. "Once." She appeared to psych herself up. "I went with a friend whose mother wanted a charm to keep her neighbor's mean tempered dog under control. The dog had bitten my friend's little brother you see, and well, the dog's owners had done nothing."

"So your friend's mother wanted something to control the mean dog?" I asked Carol. "That doesn't sound so bad."

Carol set her mug on the table. "My friend paid for the charm, and that dog died the very next day."

Despite myself, I shuddered. "It did?"

"Dropped dead." Carol snapped her fingers. "Just like that."

"So, you're saying that Irene Bishop was like a Witch for hire?" I asked wanting to be clear.

"Women from all over town paid Irene for magick. From easing the common cold to hexing their neighbors. For the right price it was understood that Irene could make your philandering husband stay home.

She'd conjure up a love spell, or even a fertility potion if you were willing to pay for it...but there were rumors that she did much worse things."

"Worse?" I tried to lighten the mood. "Did she raise an army of the shambling dead, or something?"

Carol stared at me hard. "It was whispered that one of Irene's specialties was a potion that took care of a certain *problem*, if a girl was unlucky enough to find herself in an unfortunate situation."

My stomach rolled over at the picture being painted of the woman. "Oh my goddess." *I sincerely hoped that wasn't true.* I tuned back in, right in time to hear...

"Even Silas Drake knew better than to cross Irene Bishop."

"Whoa, wait." I blinked at Carol. "What did you say?" *Silas Drake,* I hadn't heard that name before. *Probably an ancestor of Duncan's,* I supposed. I was on the verge of asking more questions when the front door opened and Sophia and Chloe Jacobs rushed in, all smiles and good cheer.

"Grandma!" the girls shouted, racing towards Carol.

Seeing a chance for a discreet exit, I took it. I texted Candice, told her I was headed home and that we could reschedule our culinary magick lessons for another time. I traveled along the neighborhood sidewalk, and before I knew it I found myself standing in front of the Drake mansion.

The old place had been renovated after the fire a few years ago, and the previous spring new landscaping had been put in. The mansion was starting to ease towards elegantly formal, instead of creepy and foreboding. But today it was the little Tudor style cottage next to it that caught my attention. It was currently available for lease, and I snickered to myself figuring it would be a long, long time before anyone in town would be brave enough to rent out the stone cottage—charming though it was—as it sat situated on the grounds of the Drake mansion.

Surrounded by old magnolia trees, it was a picturesque property. Unfortunately its neighbors made it a less than desirable spot. Almost as if my thoughts had conjured him up, Thomas Drake came marching around the side of the property flanked by two gardeners. He saw me, nodded in greeting, and kept going.

He seemed to be discussing the placement of tulip bulbs for the spring. I bit my lip, never having imagined catching such a bad-ass of a powerful sorcerer discussing the planting of the flowers in the garden. There were a few wheelbarrows full of yellow and golden brown mums to be planted, and there he was, bending down and personally selecting the mums he wanted added to the formal beds.

I supposed he was sprucing up the front gardens for the upcoming museum fundraiser, either that, or maybe he was mellowing.

I considered the stone cottage and its simple gardens as I walked along. "I'd plant pink tulips," I said to myself. "So when the magnolias bloomed in April, there'd be all those shades of pink, and the yard would look like a faery tale." I sighed as I imagined it, and a little girl raced past me on the brick sidewalk.

But she wasn't really here.

Not in this time anyway. *She hadn't happened yet,* I realized as the present faded away...

"Mama! Mama! I'm home!" she shouted happily. Her voice held the cadence of the deep South. The little girl wore a blue dress, white shoes and her hair was done in long brown pigtails. She bounded up the front steps of the cottage and into the waiting arms of a pretty brunette with pansy blue eyes.

"Love you, Sugar pie," the mother said pressing kisses to her daughter's hair. All around them the saucer magnolias bloomed in pretty soft pink and rose-colored tulips paraded along the front beds of the gardens, matching the tulips in the formal beds of the Drake's estate.

With a snap, the vision was gone, and I found myself back in the present time. The bright sunshine of early October was beaming around me, and the trees were shifting to their gorgeous fall colors. I centered myself, and reconsidered the stone cottage.

It wouldn't be empty for long. By spring there'd be a mother and child living there. I blew out a breath and started up the hill towards my home, wondering why I'd been shown the vision of the young woman and her little girl.

I let myself in the door to the bungalow and froze. My once spotless house now resembled a disaster zone. I stood stock still, staring at the mess that was all over my living room, floor and couch. It took me a moment to identify what had been chewed up and spit out as toilet paper.

Lots and lots of toilet paper. My newest roommate raced by me, swatting a nearly empty cardboard tube.

"Luna!" I said, horrified.

The cat dove under the couch, and I walked with a feeling of dread to the open door to the new downstairs bathroom. Sure enough, the toilet paper roll had been stripped off, and a puddle of paper lay on the floor. Still more shreds of toilet paper had been drug out of the bathroom and across the hardwood floors of the living room.

Somehow the cat had managed to open the antique cabinet and help herself to more rolls of paper. The glass jar filled with cotton swabs had also been knocked over. Several of those had been chewed on, and even more had been batted around the bathroom floor.

"How can one little cat make such a mess?"

"*Meow?*"

I shifted, and saw the perpetrator standing in the doorway of the bathroom with a cotton swab in her mouth and toilet paper stuck to her back paw.

"Gimme that!" I snatched the cotton swab away from her and Luna dove headfirst into the pile of toilet paper on the floor. She skidded across the floor and ended up bumping against the shower door. "You are a very bad cat," I said, trying to sound severe.

The cotton swab was all soggy from cat spit, and I immediately threw it in the garbage can. It took me a little while to get all of the toilet paper up off the floor. Both the shredded and the chewed up pieces. Luna trucked around behind me as if she were very pleased with herself. I let her keep the cardboard tubes, she really enjoyed batting those across the floor, and no sooner had the bathroom been put back to rights when I discovered the cat was sitting on the toilet seat with her head stuck in the bowl, drinking the water.

"Oh my god!" I snatched her down, shut the lid and decided I needed to figure out a way to put a latch on that glass-fronted cabinet to keep her out of any more mischief. I carted the bag of shredded and soggy paper products, and the cat, to the kitchen. I set Luna in front of her full bowl of clean water. "*This* is your water bowl," I informed her.

Luna narrowed her eyes, flipped her tail high in the air and stalked off. A knock on my back door had me turning.

Duncan was there, the afternoon sun shining down on his dark blonde hair. He wore jeans, a thin, snug orange t-shirt, and scruffy converse sneakers. Just seeing him standing there smiling at me had my heart leaping in my chest, and every muscle tightening.

Down girl, I told myself. I cleared my mind and greeted him with a casual tone. "Hi." I opened the door to let him in.

"I came by to check on you. What are you doing?" he asked.

"Cleaning up some kitty mischief." I started to tuck the bag into the retro metal kitchen can, but the can was full from last night, so I set the lid aside and began to lift out the trash bag.

"Here let me," Duncan offered, and reached for the bag.

The smell of chocolate and cherries hit us both at the same time. *The cake!* I realized too late. "Oh shit," I said. *I'd never gotten rid of the rest of that Chocolate Sin cake!*

Duncan's hands closed over the plastic bag, and his eyes jumped to mine. "You dumped the cake in the kitchen garbage can?"

"I did," I managed to say, even as the aroma became suddenly intoxicating. Some part of my brain registered that it shouldn't have still smelled like that—not *that* wonderful—especially after being discarded the evening before.

"The cake's been sitting in here all night?" Duncan snatched his hand back, and I dropped the liner back in the can. We both backed away from the metal garbage can like it was radioactive.

A light feminine laugh echoed throughout the kitchen and the overhead lights clicked off. To my amazement a pink glow began to emanate from the garbage bag.

"Uh-oh," I said as the fragrance of chocolate and cherries intensified and filled up the room.

Duncan grabbed my arm and pulled me back. He pushed me behind him, like he'd been expecting some sort of magickal explosion, or for Irene to materialize, but nothing happened. Instead the fragrance faded, and the glow melted away as if it had never been.

After a moment, I peeked out from around him. "Okay that had to be one of the weirdest—" I started to say, when Duncan leaned over and dropped his mouth on mine.

Now there was an explosion. I felt it detonate in my chest, as all the longing and lust we'd heroically squelched down the night before was ripped loose.

God I couldn't stand it! I thought. We grabbed each other and were lost. It was a battle of teeth and tongues. I nipped at his mouth and he chewed on mine. *I had to touch him, right this second.* I yanked his t-shirt up, tugged it over his head and dropped my mouth to his chest.

Those chest muscles were stronger, and more defined since the last time I'd been with him. While he held my head to his chest I sampled those pecs and cruised my mouth down to his belly. *Had to taste him, had to have him,* I thought and dropped to my knees, yanking at his belt buckle.

"Autumn," his voice was strained.

"I want you," I told him, staring up into his face. "Right now." I pulled his zipper down, tugged his briefs out of the way, and was rewarded with the proof of his desire.

"Baby, wait," he began.

"I'm not waiting anymore," I said.

Duncan let out a strangled cry as I pleasured him. He wrapped his hands in my hair while I showed him how much I had missed him, and reminded him of what we'd once shared.

"Autumn," Duncan gasped, and I smiled as I felt the tremor that ran up and down his body.

I was enjoying being the initiator, and had no intention of stopping. My hands explored his body and I delighted in the fact that I was in complete control of the moment.

I was surprised when he pulled me away from him. He yanked me to my feet, stepped out of his clothes, and hauled me to the living room. He pushed me to the sectional and I landed on my back, propped up on my elbows.

"I wasn't finished with you," I panted, reaching for him.

"I haven't even started with you yet," he said and took my glasses off. Duncan set them on an end table and turned back to me. "I'll be gentle," he said and tugged my shorts down my trembling legs. The contrast of the gruff voice and the tender motions made me clench my jaw.

"Duncan," I said through my teeth.

He paused. "Yes?"

"Don't be gentle."

He froze for a split second, and then ripped the blouse right off me.

Hearing that fabric shred made me want him even more. "Duncan!"

He dropped down and kissed me breathless. I reached for him again, but he evaded at the last second. He shoved my bra out of the way and latched onto my breast. I hissed when I felt the edge of his teeth. Duncan's fingers slid between my legs, teasing and testing, until I couldn't take the waiting any longer.

I wrapped my arms around him and rolled us off the couch. We landed with a thump on the living room floor. Duncan started to laugh until I quickly shimmied over him. The laugh became a strangled groan as I eased down, guiding him inside me. I rolled my hips, he slid even farther in, and I threw my head back shouting in triumph.

His hands covered my breasts as I began to rock. The energy danced around us, pulsing and slowly filling up the room with power. It had been a long time since I'd allowed my personal power an escape during sex. It was liberating and it only added to our pleasure. We moved together, both taking and giving generously to each other as our magicks burst free.

***

It was full dark when I woke up. Still on the living

room floor, and sprawled across Duncan's very fine chest. He was dropping tender kisses on the top of my head, and his hands were all over my ass.

"Mmmmm," I managed, and I began to nibble on his shoulder.

"Babe." Duncan sat up with me still wrapped in his arms.

"Yeah?" I murmured, sampling his shoulder.

"I want you. Again." His eyes gleamed in the dark.

"Yes," I said, pushing him back to lie on the floor.

"No." He stopped me by clamping his hands on my hips. "You had your turn being in charge."

"Yes, I did." I leaned down so we were nose to nose. "Are you going to tell me that you didn't like it?"

"Well maybe..." Duncan trailed off with a grunt when I reached down and gave him a warning squeeze. "It all happened so fast," he said in a teasing tone that had me laughing.

"Aw, you're so brave." I kissed him on the mouth. "Fought me off like a tiger, too."

"I've never known you to be so aggressive." Duncan chuckled. "I like it."

I raised an eyebrow at him. "I liked being in control."

"I noticed."

"So, what are you going to do about it?"

He stood in one motion, with me still in his arms. "Let's take this upstairs."

My breath caught from the casual display of

strength. He carried me to the stairs, and then wisely set me on my feet. I took his hand and led the way up to the second floor. I stopped in front of my room, and he pushed the door open and tugged me inside.

I squinted at the bed and back at Duncan. I couldn't see clearly without my glasses on, but as he stepped closer, the energy that radiated off of him had me gulping hard. Not sure what I'd let off the leash, I went to the bed and tugged the quilt and sheets down.

I hadn't quite straightened up when he wrapped himself around me. Now he pushed my hair out of his way and dropped kisses on the nape of my neck. His strong hands guided me to lie back on the sheets.

"Like this," he growled, arranging me as he preferred. "Stay just like this." Duncan knelt and began kissing my knees and cruising his mouth higher. I tilted my hips back and helplessly higher as he teased me with his mouth, never quite landing where I needed him the most.

"Duncan!" I demanded.

Finally he stopped tormenting me and I let out a little shriek as his tongue licked and stabbed at my core. He nudged my legs farther apart, and didn't let go until I was shouting from my own release. I tried to catch my breath as he climbed up over me. My heart was racing when he pulled me close, and thrust home.

"God, I've missed you." I heard him say.

All I could manage was a strangled gasp. His pace was leisurely at first. Soon that changed when I began to move helplessly against him. Duncan pulled my legs up higher, and it pressed him even deeper inside. The feeling was incredible. I wrapped my legs around him and hung on for dear life.

And I discovered something. Allowing him to set the tone and pace was every bit as exciting as being in control myself.

***

I sat soaking in the warm water of the claw footed tub in the upstairs bathroom. Bubbles floated across the surface of the water, and soft Celtic music played in the background. My back was resting against Duncan's chest and I reclined in his arms, totally content. There were several candles flickering in glass votive holders on the counter, and the atmosphere was decadent and romantic.

It was only me, Duncan—and the cat. Luna sat on the closed lid of the toilet and stared, as if she wasn't quite sure what to make of us.

"This is a great old tub," Duncan said.

I tipped my head back to grin at him. "I'm becoming rather fond of it myself."

"How are you feeling?" Duncan asked.

"Relaxed, happy," I sighed. "And you?"

"The same."

"We controlled our magick," I said. "Mostly."

"I don't think we blew anything up that first time on

the living room floor."

"I sure hope not," I said wryly. "I just finished the reno."

Duncan laughed at that. "Well, if we did, I'll fix it for you."

I rested my head against his shoulder. "There wasn't even a single flicker of a light bulb. I'd say we've gained some control of our sexual energies when they combine."

"Remember our very first time?" Duncan wiggled his eyebrows at me.

"Yeah," I sighed. "We blew up lights, *and* fried the clock."

"Those were the days," Duncan said, and that made me laugh until he silenced me with a lengthy kiss.

We lingered in the bath, and once the water cooled we reluctantly got out. I slipped a robe on, and Duncan came downstairs with a towel slung low over his hips. I put my glasses back on, and grinned when I saw our clothes scattered all over the floor of the kitchen and living room. I picked them up and handed Duncan his shorts.

Duncan got dressed and immediately carried the bag containing that leftover cake out back to add to the outdoor trash cans. He went directly to the sink and washed his hands thoroughly afterwards, and I put a few sandwiches together and we sat at the kitchen table, eating a late dinner. Afterwards we cuddled on the couch and I asked him to stay.

Without a word, he stood and held out a hand. We went straight upstairs and back to my bed.

CHAPTER SIX

As the sun came up Sunday morning we lingered over a goodbye kiss on the back porch. I would have liked him to stay for the day, but I had an appointment at the museum at eleven o'clock. I waved as Duncan headed towards his truck and couldn't help but wonder how the family would react to the news of Duncan and I being back together.

When I arrived at the museum's meeting room I met with Olivia before the other Historical Society members arrived to deliver the flyers I'd designed for the upcoming fundraiser. I was happy to help her out, as I genuinely liked the older woman. We'd spent several lunch breaks talking about gardening over the past year at the museum.

I'd only began to ease out of the way of the meeting when I was stopped by one of the elderly members. "Oh." She peered up at me through thick glasses. "You're the new Bishop girl."

"Yes, ma'am," I answered politely. It didn't seem to

matter that I'd lived in William's Ford for four years, I was still to the locals—the 'new' Bishop girl.

The woman patted her curly white hair. "You're the one who bought the yellow bungalow, that house that belonged to Irene, aren't you?"

"Yes ma'am, I did."

"You taking up where Irene left off?"

Her sly words had my stomach roiling. "Excuse me?"

The woman sent me a crafty smile. "Well, you know, that Irene Bishop, she had *power*," she said.

Before I could work up a polite response, Olivia stepped forward. "Mabel, why are you pestering Autumn?"

Mabel adjusted her thin sweater over her shoulders. "I'm not pestering her, I'm only curious."

"Autumn." Olivia latched onto my arm and began to steer me away. "I was wondering if you'd help me bring out the snacks."

"Sure."

We stepped through to the kitchenette off the meeting room. "I'm sorry about that," Olivia said quietly. "Mabel Watkins is a gossipmonger and completely rude."

"Well, I have to admit that she caught me off guard." I headed towards a tray of cookies and lifted them.

"I suppose it was only a matter of time before someone asked you," Olivia said, hefting a tray of pastries.

I frowned. "Before someone asked me what?"

Olivia stopped and met my eyes. "Whether or not you were going to be following in your ancestor's footsteps."

"I'm not sure what you mean," I said, deliberately playing dumb.

"Your great-aunt, she was a miracle worker." Olivia's voice was sincere, and I was shocked at the difference in her description of Irene as compared to Carol Jacobs' from the day before.

"A miracle worker?" I repeated.

Olivia beamed up at me. "Why if not for her, my sister would have never had any children."

"I'm sorry, I'm not following you," I said cautiously. "Did she recommend a doctor or something?"

"Please don't insult my intelligence." Olivia huffed out a little breath. "I understand that you'd be discreet when it comes to your family, but sweetie, you don't have to hide anything from me."

"I see." And I was starting to. *Olivia knew about the legacy of magick.* I read the woman, checking her aura. It was shimmering in a vibrant shade of orange. "So you're claiming that Irene helped your sister in some way?"

"I'm not claiming anything. I'm stating facts. Irene worked miracles for my sister. I know, because I was there."

"I'd love to hear about that," I said and took the heavy tray from her. "I have very little first-hand information about the woman."

Olivia nudged the door open with her hip. "And I bet what you have heard hasn't been very complimentary."

"Not so far," I admitted.

Olivia shook her head. "People are often afraid of what they don't understand."

The phrase so often used by Witches had me reconsidering her. "Are you a practitioner, Olivia?"

"Me?" Olivia chuckled. "No, I'm a mundane."

I smiled at the older woman. "Your aura doesn't read like one. Are you sure you don't have any gifts?"

"Well I've got my feminine intuition, and I figure that's more than some folks ever even think to use."

I followed her towards the conference room. "Olivia, why don't you drop by my house after the meeting and we can talk?" I invited her. "I'd like to hear about your experiences."

"I'd enjoy that," Olivia said as she entered the meeting room. The noise of a couple dozen people swelled. "Give me a couple hours and I'll be over."

I set the trays down on the table and nodded at Olivia. "Perfect, I'll see you later." Leaving the historical society to their meeting, I went up to my own office.

***

I was sitting on the bench on my front porch in jeans and a casual t-shirt when Olivia whipped her compact car into my driveway. Cheerfully, she exclaimed over the front gardens, and I ushered her inside and gave her a little tour. I couldn't help but chuckle over her excitement to see the renovations to the bungalow. We settled at the kitchen table, and Luna hopped right up into her lap as I brewed my guest a cup of tea.

Luna preened over the attention while Olivia made kissy noises over the cat. "I have something for you," she said fishing inside of her handbag.

I accepted a five by seven inch photo from Olivia. It was an old black and white picture. I studied the group of twelve people posing so formally. "Who's this?"

"This is a photo of the members of the Historical Society from 1965," Olivia explained. "Your great-aunt Irene is in the photo, along with some members from the other *significant* families in William's Ford."

I raised my eyebrows at her emphasis on the word. "Significant?"

"Yes." Olivia took the photo back. She pointed to Irene, and I marveled at seeing the woman in her late thirties. She, like her sister Faye, were striking women. Her chin was lifted and I caught the impression of both elegance and pride.

"She was beautiful," I said.

"She truly was." Olivia pointed to the photo again. "See the men standing next to her?"

I tucked my hair behind my ear. "The nice looking guy with the beard?"

"That's Phillip Drake," Olivia said, sliding her finger

over farther to the right. "And here is his brother, Silas Drake."

Silas Drake. I jolted. *Even Silas Drake was cautious of Irene,* Carol Jacobs' voice played back in my mind. "These Drake men," I began, "are ancestors of Thomas Drake, I assume?"

"You assume correctly," Olivia said. "Silas was Thomas Drake's father."

I studied the photo of Duncan's grandfather and great-uncle. Silas had dark hair and eyes, and I saw some resemblance to Thomas. While Phillip was more classically handsome, as a matter of fact he reminded me a little of Julian. But Silas...there was something shadowy there, even his photo gave me the creeps.

"I can see some similarities to the modern day Drakes." I tried to sound casual, even as I rejoiced that Duncan didn't resemble either of the men.

"I thought you might enjoy having a photo of Irene," Olivia said. "I found this the other day, and wondered why I felt compelled to make a copy of it. Now I know why."

"Thank you." I set the photo down on the table.

"But let's get to the real reason why I'm here." Olivia rubbed her hands together. "You want to know more about Irene and her...activities."

I sat and listened as Olivia told me the story of her older sister, who'd tried for years to conceive and had been told it would be impossible. In the early spring of 1975, Olivia and her sister Jane had visited the bungalow. Irene had held her hands over Jane's belly, listening carefully as Jane explained all the tests she'd had and how the doctors hadn't given her any hope.

"So your Aunt Irene told my sister that she could increase her chances of conceiving but that the fertility magick would be costly."

"Costly?" I asked.

"Yes." Olivia nodded. "Jane had to pay her in cash. Three thousand dollars."

I whistled through my teeth. "That was a good chunk of change back them."

"In today's money that'd be the equivalent of over thirteen K," Olivia agreed.

"Yowsers." I blinked at her quick calculation.

"I've been married to an accountant for forty years." Olivia grinned. "I know money. So where was I?" Olivia asked herself. "Oh, right. My sister paid her in cash. Irene gave Jane the potions and cast her magick for her."

"And it worked?" I asked.

"It did. Jane became pregnant shortly after that. My nephew was born ten months from the day Jane had paid for that spell."

I nodded politely, even as I wondered what working that sort of magick had physically cost Irene. Pulling off something that 'big' would have taken a heavy toll on the caster.

Olivia continued with her tale. Now it was 1980 and Jane wanted a second child. "So Jane came back?" I asked, trying to keep up with the story.

"She did, and again I came with her." Olivia leaned forward getting into the re-telling. "I was eight months pregnant with my son, and Irene made me sit down and put my feet up. She gave me seven sorts of hell about staying off my feet, unless I wanted the baby to come early." Olivia chuckled over the memory. "She made me chamomile tea and fed me cookies. Even sent me home with an herbal sachet to help me relax."

"That was nice," I said.

"I told you." Olivia pointed at me. "Irene Bishop was an angel. And to your aunt's credit she did warn Jane that if she worked the fertility spell for her again, that it would take a heavy toll on my sister's health."

So she fussed over an expectant mother, and had tried to warn Jane, I thought. This didn't quite fit with the image Carol Jacobs had painted of a woman doling out baneful magicks that put the whammy on philandering husbands, and eliminated mean-tempered dogs.

"But Jane desperately wanted another baby," Olivia said. "And this time the price was five thousand dollars. In cash."

I exhaled. "Prices had gone up."

"My sister conceived within three months. But the pregnancy was difficult. She was restricted to bed rest for the last trimester, and even then, we almost lost them both."

Despite myself, I was curious. "What happened?"

"Placenta abruption," Olivia replied. "It was touch and go for a while. They did an emergency C-section, and then my sister had to have a hysterectomy at the age of thirty two."

"Wow," I managed. "Did she blame Irene?"

"No she didn't." Olivia shook her head. "As a matter of fact your great-aunt came and sat with me and my brother-in-law at the hospital. Irene held my hand while we waited, and she prayed with us."

Moved, I wiped tears from my eyes. "This story about Irene is quite the contrast from my other source of information."

"Your aunt *was* a miracle worker. And nothing anyone could ever say would convince me otherwise," Olivia said, taking her cell phone out of her purse. "I want to show you something." She held up the phone. "This is a picture of my niece, she's thirty-six years old now and has children of her own."

I studied the photo of the young woman with brown hair, and the happy smile. "She's lovely," I told Olivia.

"Her name is Melissa," Olivia said as she tucked her phone away. "Melissa Irene."

***

After Olivia left I couldn't settle down, so I did some laundry. I changed the sheets on my bed and tossed them in the washer, put a load of towels in the dryer, and I hung up a few dresses to air dry on a bar in the basement. I went up to the second bedroom I'd been using as a home office and decided to document my conversation with Olivia. I opened a new file and wrote down the tale of Jane and her babies, and also everything I could remember from talking to Carol Jacobs.

I eyeballed the bulletin board above my desk and was inspired to create a timeline of everything I knew about Irene Bishop. I took a sticky note, wrote 1965 on it and tacked it on the side of the photo Olivia had given me. I placed it at the top of the bulletin board.

Thanks to the paperwork from the house sale, I knew Irene had taken over ownership of the bungalow in 1967. According to Aunt Faye, Irene had added the fence that divided the properties—shortly thereafter. I made another note about the bungalow coming into Irene's care and the fence addition, dated that 1967-1968 and stuck that under the photo. Finally, I wrote out two more notes entitled: 1975 Jane's baby #1 and 1980 Jane's baby #2 also arranging them beneath the photo Olivia had given me.

I added four more notes. One listing the year that Irene had passed away. Another for the year that the Greenes purchased the bungalow. Next, I added the date of my purchase of the bungalow, and finally, the date I took possession of the house, when we found the cookbook.

It wasn't much of a timeline, but it was all I had…so far. I started an internet search, hoping to find more photos of Irene, or perhaps some news. After an hour searching, I came across a few mentions of her being a member of the Historical Society, and I found an old article from 1967 that mentioned Irene attending a fundraiser for a new library being built at the University.

There was a grainy newspaper photo of her standing next to Phillip Drake, along with a few other people. I printed out the article and the photo, wrote 1967 across the top, and added it to the bulletin board next to the note about when she'd taken possession of the bungalow.

I studied the old newspaper photo. It was certainly interesting that the two photos of Irene as a younger woman both had Phillip Drake in them.

"Coincidence or not?" I wondered, deciding to do a search on Phillip Drake.

Phillip had been the older of the two brothers. He had been an English professor at the University. He'd never married and had passed away in 1968 after a lingering illness at the age of forty-three. I turned back to his photos. He'd been a handsome man. I wonder if Irene had grieved for him. Had they been friends, or acquaintances? Or merely fellow Historical Society members? "Or maybe you're grasping at straws," I muttered.

I began an internet search on Silas, and learned that the man had been a mover and a shaker back in his day. He'd been on the board of the University, and had even served as the president of the Alumni Association for several years. He'd been in real estate, apparently successful, and from what I could tell he must have added to his family's fortune. I found his obituary, and to my surprise Silas Drake had passed away at some upscale nursing home only a year ago at the age of ninety.

"Huh," I said. "I hadn't even known Duncan's grandfather had been alive." Luna jumped up on my desk and began to nose around my pencil holder. "Well he lived a good long life, anyway," I decided.

A loud bang and thudding sound had me jumping in my chair. I leapt to my feet and sped downstairs. Realizing the noise was coming from the basement I ran across the kitchen, yanked open the basement door, and clattered down the steps. "Stupid washing machine," I muttered. Almost every time I did a larger load of laundry the old machine went out of balance, making a hell of a racket.

I slapped the buttons to stop the spin cycle, opened the lid and reached in to rearrange the sheets in the basket. I was about to turn the machine back on when the smell of burning rubber hit me. I yanked the washing machine's plug out of the wall, and the dryer's for good measure.

On cue the basement smoke detector began to go off, and I saw a little puff of smoke coming up from the back of the dryer. "What the hell?" I said as the smoke intensified and the alarms continued to shrill. *The dryer was burning,* I realized, *and my fire extinguisher was in the kitchen.* Frightened, I raced back up the stairs for it.

"No, no, no!" I chanted, rushing back downstairs. "Don't do this to me now!" I pulled the pin, aimed, getting one good shot out of it. There was a second half-hearted one, then it fizzled and was done. Disgusted, I dropped the metal canister, and discovered that the dryer was now pouring smoke. I started coughing as the smoke began rolling out from around where the vent ran up the paneled wall and out of the basement window.

"Shit!" I reached for my cell phone in my back pocket.

I dialed 911. "This is Autumn Bishop," I said over the smoke detector alarm. "The dryer is on fire in my basement!"

I gave the operator my address, and went back upstairs, away from the smoke and closed the basement door behind me. When the operator calmly suggested I get out of the house and remove any pets, I panicked, and hung up. I ran around calling for the cat, eventually finding her asleep on my office chair. I threw a blanket over her, wrapped her up like a kitty burrito, and lifted her. I grabbed my purse off my bedroom dresser, ran down the steps and out the front door.

I stood on the front porch while the cat struggled against the blanket. Luna wailed, her little head sticking out, and she glared at me while I waited for the fire department. "Duncan had only just finished the renovations, and now this!" I said to Luna, as my heart pounded.

Thinking of him, I shot off a quick, one handed text to Duncan: *The dryer caught fire. I'm ok. Fire Dept. on the way.*

I hit 'send' and it occurred to me that I should call the family too, but I never got the chance. I heard the fire truck come roaring up the hill, sirens blaring and lights flashing. The truck pulled up in front of the bungalow as Bran, Lexie, Holly, little Morgan, and Aunt Faye came racing over across the yard from next door.

"What happened?" Bran yelled.

"Are you okay?" Lexie called as she ran with Belinda in her arms.

"I'm okay!" I called to them as they rushed through the opening in the fence between the yards. "The dryer in the basement caught fire."

Lexie bounded up the stairs, took me by the arm and pulled me off the porch and out into the yard. "Come on, you'll need to get out of the way."

Bran was steps behind his wife. "I've got her," he said to his wife.

"I'm not hurt, Bran," I insisted. While Lexie began speaking to the firefighters, Holly eased up and took Belinda.

"It's in the basement," I said to one of the firefighters, "I'll show you."

"No you won't," Bran said, tightening his grip on

my arm. "Morgan John," Bran called to his son. "Take Autumn's cat back to our house."

"I can take care of the kitty," Morgan insisted, reaching for Luna.

I nodded, handed him the blanket-wrapped cat and gave my attention to the fireman. I showed the firefighters into the house, took them to the basement door, and Bran nudged me out of the way so the emergency responders could do their thing.

I was escorted back across the porch in time to see Morgan carrying the cat across the back patio of the manor, with Aunt Faye supervising. Holly was right behind them with Belinda. Lexie clamped onto my arm, tugged me down the steps and out across the lawn towards the fence. I stood there dumbfounded as more men began to drag a hose through the house.

"Oh my goddess," I sniffled. "Please don't let there be too much damage."

Duncan arrived a few minutes later. He parked across the street and leapt out of his truck. My jaw dropped when I saw that Thomas was with him.

Duncan rushed over the grass. "You're okay?"

"I told you I was." I assured him. "The dryer was second hand," I explained. "The old set was left behind by the Greenes."

Thomas Drake nodded at the family as we stood on the lawn. "How bad is the fire?"

"Hopefully not too bad," I said, doing my best not to gawk at him.

Duncan pulled me close and wrapped his arm around my shoulders. "I hate fires," he muttered.

"I tried to put it out myself," I said, leaning against him a little more. "But my fire extinguisher didn't work very well. The smoke started getting heavy so I called the fire department."

"That was quick thinking," Thomas said. "I'm happy that you are alright."

"Thank you." I tried to ignore Bran's raised eyebrows at Thomas Drake's presence, and Lexie's grin at Duncan and I standing together.

"You have homeowner's insurance, I assume?" Thomas asked.

"Yes, of course," I said.

"Excellent." Thomas nodded at Bran and Lexie. "How are your children?" he asked conversationally.

Lexie put her hand on Bran's arm, a subtle reminder to be polite. "They're fine, and safe next door with Holly and Aunt Faye watching over them."

"The new baby, it's a girl, correct?" Thomas said to my brother and sister-in-law.

"Yes, a girl," Bran's expression softened. "We named her Belinda."

Maybe it was the strain, but I felt like I'd passed into a parallel universe. There stood Thomas Drake and my brother and sister-in-law, having a polite, albeit slightly stiff conversation—while my basement was on fire.

A firefighter called me over. He explained that they had the fire out, and were hauling the old dryer up the basement stairs and out the back door to get the burnt appliance out of the house.

"The dryer is the number one cause of house fires," the firefighter said. "Your dryer looked old and it was likely the lint in the vent hose or the filter that caught."

I gulped. "How bad is it?"

"Come with me, and I'll show you the damage." The firefighter led the way, and without thinking, I kept ahold of Duncan's hand and tugged him along with me. I wrinkled my nose at the acrid smell of smoke that lingered in the house.

I'd been lucky. While the fire extinguisher hadn't been a good one, it had apparently taken the fire down a little. The floor was wet from the fire hose. There were burn marks on the painted paneling where the dryer had stood, and a few holes had been punched through the paneling from where the firefighters had checked to make sure nothing else was on fire. I could see a few studs and the concrete walls through the holes. The washing machine was black on one side. The basement stunk of smoke but the little windows were open, and I hoped the smell would dissipate.

Clearly I was going to have to call a clean-up crew, *and* find a way to finance a new washer and dryer. It was also firmly suggested that I have a new dryer and venting professionally installed. I listened to the firefighters and was very grateful that Duncan was there to ask more questions. To be honest my head was spinning, all I could think was how expensive it would be to buy a new washer and dryer, and to pay for the clean-up and repairs to the basement.

I would be able to stay in the house, but I wanted to open up every window immediately and air it out. The living room furniture wasn't even a week old, I hope it wouldn't smell like smoke.

"I can have a clean-up crew here tomorrow," Duncan said as we went back up the stairs.

I tried not to cringe at the mess the hose had left across my hardwood floors and kitchen tile. "Thank you," I managed, and to my embarrassment, tears began to spill over.

CHAPTER SEVEN

After the firefighters left, I called my insurance company, reported the fire and took a bunch of pictures. With the windows open and a few box fans running, the smell on the main and second floor wasn't too bad. The basement reeked, however. Ivy and Nathan showed up and along with Holly and Bran, they helped me wipe up the floors on the main level. We scrubbed up the kitchen and the new bathroom, which helped to alleviate the smoky smell. Once the kids were down for the night, Lexie brought Luna back over, and everyone began to trickle home.

Eventually it was down to me, Duncan, Ivy and Nathan. Ivy insisted on spending the night, and she walked Nathan out to his car, which allowed Duncan and me a chance to kiss goodnight.

"I'm glad Ivy is staying with you tonight," Duncan said, holding me in his arms.

"The dryer is out in the yard. I'm safe." I gave him a squeeze. "If anything else hinky goes on, I'll call you, right away."

"You'd better." Duncan kissed me again. "I'll call you in the morning."

"Thanks for being here," I said. We walked to the door, and I stood on the front porch waiting as he drove away. Ivy came bouncing up the steps a few moments later.

"So," Ivy began, "you and Duncan hooked up."

"I didn't say that we did."

Ivy gave me a little hip bump. "You don't have to say anything, you still project your emotions."

"No I don't," I insisted. "I have that under control these days."

Ivy snorted. "Keep telling yourself that. I picked up on your emotions from out in the driveway."

"You did? From the driveway?"

"Yeah, I did." Ivy patted my arm. "Plus I watched you both while we cleaned up. He's acting more like the Duncan we first met, and even with everything that happened today, you seem happy. Happier than I've seen you in a long time."

"Oh," was about all I could manage.

"I always wondered how long it would take you two to find your way back together."

I sighed, not quite ready to examine my feelings too closely.

"So this has been pretty recent, eh?" Ivy asked. "Surprised you both?"

"Yes."

"Gimme the details."

"Do I butt into your personal life, Ivy?"

"Yes, you do, and I know you would again if you thought I needed it. Because that's what families do."

I slung my arm around her shoulders. "I'm glad you're staying tonight."

"Come on." Ivy put her arm around my waist. "Let's get you cleaned up. You smell like smoke."

I headed for the new downstairs bathroom and hit the showers. When I shut off the water I saw that Ivy had taken my clothes, and had left a couple of blue towels from the upstairs bath sitting out for me. I wrapped myself in one towel, dried my hair with the second and went upstairs.

"Thanks for the fresh towels," I said, walking back in my room.

"No problem." Ivy sat in the middle of my bed with Luna in her lap. "When we scrubbed up the main floor I noticed the pink downstairs towels smelled smoky so I had Lexie take them over to the manor to wash them."

I reached for a brush on my dresser. "Oh, well thanks."

"I put your clothes in a plastic bag," Ivy said. "We can wash those and anything else tomorrow."

I sighed. "Yeah I'll be doing a lot of laundry tomorrow." I suddenly realized I'd lost an entire load of towels, and the sheets that had been in the washer. My stomach gave a nasty pitch, when I recalled the dresses I'd had air drying down in the basement. *I'd never get the smell out of those.* I'd loved those dresses, and they were ruined now. I tried to remind myself that the damage was minimal and I was lucky.

Ivy sniffed the air. "Do you smell that?"

"What?" Alarmed, I dropped my brush. "Do you smell smoke again?"

"No," Ivy said, inhaling deeply. "I smell lilacs."

"Oh." Mentally, I pried my fingernails out of the ceiling.

"It's like it's coming in through the windows, but that can't be right. It's October." Ivy frowned. "And lilacs only bloom in the spring. Not during the fall."

I picked up the brush. "That's Irene's calling card, remember? I usually catch the scent of lilacs when she's floating around the bungalow."

Ivy pursed her lips. "Did you smell lilacs before the dryer caught fire this afternoon?"

"No, but the wash machine went out of balance and was thudding pretty loudly. I got up and went to the basement to fix it and..." I trailed off as realization dawned.

"And you were down there in time to keep the fire from getting too bad," Ivy said. "Maybe that was Irene trying to warn you."

A little breeze had my bedroom curtains fluttering, and the fragrance of lilacs intensified. "Well if so, thanks, Aunt Irene," I said.

Ivy sniffed the air again. "It's fading now."

"I guess she's done for the day." I shrugged and went

back to brushing out my hair.

"You're taking the whole ghost-in-my-house thing like a champ," Ivy said.

I finished my hair. "Well I had plenty of practice with Grandma Rose at the manor, didn't I?"

"Grandma Rose showed herself to me last year, right around Samhain," Ivy said. "Did I ever tell you that?"

"No, you didn't."

"She sort of popped up after Nathan and I almost..."

"Almost?" When Ivy grinned at me, I put it together. "Oh, *almost*. I see."

Ivy wiggled her eyebrows. "She startled me pretty good, embarrassed me a little. Made me wonder how long she'd been hanging around, and what all she had *seen*."

"Oh lord," I muttered.

"Yeah well, never a dull moment with the Bishop family."

"We're an exciting bunch of Witches, alright," I said. "Cursed grimoires, haunted dormitories, bewitched amethyst brooches, family ghosts, and basement fires."

"Hey, in all the excitement, I forgot to tell you. I got a phone call from Hannah yesterday," Ivy said, speaking of Nathan's sister. "She and Henry are engaged."

"Good for her." I grabbed a night shirt and some underwear and got ready for bed while I listened to Ivy chatter happily about the couple and their engagement.

"Henry gave her an emerald ring," Ivy said, pulling

her phone out of her back pocket. "Here, check this out. She sent me a picture."

I took the phone and couldn't help but smile at the picture on Ivy's phone. The happy couple stood embracing. Hannah's left hand rested on Henry's chest, the ring in plain view. Tucked under the man's arm, a blonde little boy grinned up at his mother.

"Nice ring," I said, admiring the deep green oval stone surrounded by a halo of tiny diamonds. "I've always liked colored stones."

Ivy took back the phone and grinned down at the picture. "Eli is so happy. Nathan's nephew is a great little kid."

"He's a cutie," I agreed and gathered up the towels, and hung them up on hooks behind the bathroom door.

"I've been trying to talk them into coming out here for a visit, Thanksgiving maybe," Ivy said as I came back in.

"That'd be nice. I'd like to meet Hannah and Eli," I said, stifling a yawn. "Oh, and Henry too."

"You'd like them." She got up and set Luna aside. Neatly, Ivy began to fold back the quilt on the bed. "Can I borrow a nightshirt?"

"Sure," I said, shifting towards the dresser. "Let me get you one." I took a step, tripped on the rug and caught myself.

"Autumn." Ivy frowned at me. "Go to bed, I can find what I need." She steered me towards my bed, gave me a nudge. "Your mother should have named you Grace."

I wrinkled my nose. "I suppose my father had a hand in my name, it's subtly witchy, naming me after the season I was born in." I yawned and dropped my phone on the area rug.

"Give me that!" Ivy sighed, bent over and scooped up the phone. "Get in bed before you hurt yourself."

"Are you gonna tuck me in, too?" I couldn't resist snarking as I climbed in.

"I might if it will keep you from crashing into something else."

Ivy walked over to my dresser and began rooting around. While I took off my glasses and plugged my phone in to re-charge, she made herself at home. She stripped down, tossed her clothes towards the bench at the foot of the bed, and pulled an oversized t-shirt on. The next thing I knew the overhead lights went out and my cousin was climbing in bed, snuggling right up beside me.

"It's like old times," she giggled. "Roomie."

I chuckled, remembering when she'd bunked with me at the manor for a few months. I tried to ease over a bit, but that only made her cuddle up closer. "You never did comprehend the concept of personal space."

"Aw, don't be such a hard ass." Ivy shivered. "It's starting to get a little chilly."

"Maybe I'm not used to having someone right up against me when I'm trying to go to sleep," I groused.

"Don't you cuddle with Duncan?" Ivy asked. "Nathan and I cuddle together afterwards."

I stared at the darkened ceiling, and gave up. "We haven't had much opportunity for cuddling afterwards."

"Oh, so you're a couple of wild animals, eh?" Ivy waited a beat. "So, first time back together...Did you tear each other's clothes off?"

Damned intuitives. I was suddenly very grateful that the room was dark, because I was sure I was blushing. "I am not discussing the details of my sex life with you, Ivy."

"Why?" Ivy wanted to know. "So was Duncan all romantic, tender and slow, or did he yank your hair back and ravage you like a lusty pirate?"

Despite myself I burst out laughing. "You did *not* just say, 'ravage you like a lusty pirate'."

"There's nothing wrong with a good romp in the boudoir," Ivy insisted.

"By the goddess." I glanced over at her. "I didn't know you were a bodice-ripper-romance-novel fan, Ivy."

"Sure." Ivy grinned, I could see her face in the dark. "Those books are *hot*."

I shut my eyes. "I'm way too tired for this conversation."

"You can borrow some of my romance novels if you like. Maybe they will inspire you." Ivy sounded completely serious.

"Ah, no," I said. "I'm fine, thanks." I tried not to laugh again. It would only encourage her.

Ivy patted my thigh. "Get some sleep." She rolled

over away from me and Luna jumped up on the bed. The calico climbed up Ivy's side and settled on her hip.

"Night, Shorty," I said.

"I'm not short," Ivy insisted.

I yawned and answered as I always did. "You're shorter than me."

***

Monday morning dawned, and I woke to find Ivy had curled up in a little ball on her side of the bed with the sheet up over her head. Luna was wedged between the two of us, and there was a definite nip of fall coming in through the open windows. I shivered and reached for the blankets at the foot of the bed, dragging a quilt up over us all.

Beside me on the night stand, my phone chimed. I reached out, snagged it, and pulled the phone under the covers with me.

It was a text from Duncan: *Morning. I have a cleaning crew scheduled to arrive at 8:30 am.*

I squinted at the screen and re-read the message. I sent back: *That was fast.*

He responded quickly: *See you soon.*

I checked the time. It was 7:32. I couldn't believe I'd slept so long. I hadn't slept past 5:30 in years. I scrolled through my contacts, and sent a quick text to Professor Meyer, informing him I was taking a personal day.

Ivy stirred beside me. "Are you really sending texts

at zero dark thirty?" Her voice was muffled from under the covers.

"It's after seven thirty," I said. "The sun is up."

"God, I always hated the fact that you woke up so freaking early."

"The clean-up crew will be here in less than an hour," I warned her.

Ivy's response was a muffled groan.

"Don't you have classes today?"

"Not till after eleven," Ivy said, still under the covers. "Because I'm allergic to mornings."

"Like the good little vampire you are." I sat up and reached for my glasses.

"Now who's using romance novel metaphors?"

I rolled out of bed, saw her burrowed under the blankets and couldn't resist teasing her. "You don't call Nathan *Vlad* in moments of passion do you?"

Ivy pulled the covers down to her chin. "Only if he calls me Mina," she said, deadpan. "And our safety word, is garlic."

I burst out laughing, and Ivy pulled the covers back up over her head. I went downstairs to the kitchen to make some tea, grinning the whole way.

Ivy made the supreme sacrifice of gracing me with her presence a short time later. She shuffled down to the kitchen in her jeans and t-shirt from yesterday. "Caffeine," she muttered with her eyes half closed. "Don't make me hurt you."

Knowing her personal preference for soda in the

morning, I set down my bowl of cereal and went to the fridge to hand her a chilled can. "Do you want me to drop you back on campus?" I asked when she came up from chugging.

"Nathan said he'd pick me up at 8:30." Ivy took another swig. "That way I can hit the showers and change before class." She burped, loud and long.

"You're welcome to take a shower here." I dug back into my cereal as Luna chomped on her kibble.

Ivy snapped her head around. "I can use the new, fancy downstairs shower?"

"Sure. There's hair products and a hair dryer in the pink cabinet."

"I'll go grab some towels from the upstairs bathroom." Ivy set her soft drink down and dashed back to the second floor.

I chuckled at seeing her move so quickly, especially in the morning. She zipped by me again and the untouched bathroom door shut behind her. I ate my breakfast and went back upstairs to get dressed before the clean-up crew arrived.

An hour later and Ivy was ready for the day after having borrowed a t-shirt of mine and helping herself to some of my cosmetics. While I worked on a second cup of tea, she sat at the kitchen table, texting Nathan.

"Would you like some cereal or something?" I asked her.

"No thanks," she said. "Nathan is taking me out to breakfast."

"See? There are benefits to getting up early."

Ivy rolled her eyes and kept texting.

A knock on the kitchen door had us both turning. Duncan stood there smiling at me through the glass.

"Good morning—" I began, opening the door. I never had the chance to say anything else, because he stepped over the threshold and pulled me into his arms for a thorough kiss.

For a few moments I forgot about everything else, then the sound of clapping had us breaking apart.

"Now that's how you start the morning!" Ivy cheered, making me chuckle.

"Hey, Shorty." Duncan grinned at her.

Ivy beamed at us. "Hey yourself."

Duncan tipped my chin up to study my face. "Was everything quiet last night?"

I frowned. "Why wouldn't it have been?"

"I wondered if Irene had put in an appearance," Duncan said.

"We smelled lilacs last night," I said. "But that was it."

"Yeah," Ivy piped up. "I think maybe the washing machine going out of balance was caused by Irene—as a way to get Autumn down to the basement in time to see that the dryer was catching fire."

"Interesting theory." Duncan nodded to Ivy.

"I'll ask Nathan about it," Ivy decided. "He's the expert on ghosts."

"That's probably a good idea," I said.

Ivy narrowed her eyes. "Come to think of it, he did mention to me that he thought you had more of an intelligent haunt than a residual one."

"Intelligent haunt?" Duncan shifted to stand beside me. "Do you mean interactive?"

"Yeah," Ivy said. "He'll probably want to interview you both. Get your first hand experiences."

I nodded in agreement. "I suppose I should bring in an expert, especially considering everything that's been going on around here."

Ivy perked up. "You're holding something back." She looked from me and back to Duncan. "Something about chocolate? Ooh, and my intuition tells me that it's *important*."

"It's personal, Ivy," I said, trying to stall.

Thankfully there was a knock on the front door. "Come in, Nathan," I called.

"Good morning," Nathan said as he came into the kitchen. He'd always been serious and intense, but now that he and Ivy were a couple, his expression was often softer.

Ivy bounced up. "I'll talk to him, and see how soon we can come over."

Nathan's horizontal brows drew together. "What are you plotting, Ivy?"

Ivy reached up and kissed Nathan. "A little paranormal investigation here at the bungalow," she explained.

"I do have some theories on that," Nathan said. "Let

me check my schedule. I'll call you later and we can set something up."

I smiled at him. "Thanks Nathan."

After Nathan and Ivy left to go out for breakfast, I made a cup of coffee for Duncan. The sun was shining and Luna sat in the open window watching the birds in the garden through the screen.

"How did things go with Ivy, last night?" he wanted to know.

"Fine," I said, handing him his coffee. "But she did ask me what kind of lover you were. Style wise."

Duncan paused in mid sip. "She did?" His eyes grew wide.

I tucked my tongue in my cheek. "Yeah, she wanted to know if you were all tender and slow. *Or* if you yanked my hair back and ravaged me like a lusty pirate."

Duncan choked on his coffee and then roared with laughter.

I grinned at him. "Seems my cousin has a predilection for romance novels."

"I don't know whether I'm complimented or embarrassed that she asked."

"It's Ivy," I reminded him. "She's incorrigible."

Duncan set his mug aside and caged me in at the counter with his arms. "A lusty pirate, eh?" he asked, leaning in close.

"Aye, Captain," I said, playfully fluttering my lashes at him.

"I'm putting 'ravishing you like a lusty pirate', on my to-do list." Duncan said in a tone that had my insides quaking.

"She also offered to let me borrow her romance novels in case I needed some more inspiration."

"I've always liked that girl," Duncan decided, and slowly reached for the buttons on my denim shirt. He unbuttoned them one by one, his eyes never leaving mine. "I want you, Autumn."

"I want you too," I said, leaning forward to kiss him. "I missed you last night."

Duncan pushed my shirt aside and ran his hands over me. "Think we have enough time before the cleaning crew gets here? I could start working on that to-do list."

I was on the verge of suggesting we run upstairs when I got a flash in my mind of the cleaning crew pulling up outside. "Time just ran out," I said, pulling back from him and buttoning my shirt.

Duncan groaned. "Figures."

***

The morning was spent answering texts and concerned phone calls from my friends, and trying to keep Luna out of the way as the cleaning crew got to work. They used some sort of upholstery cleaner on the new sectional sofa, and whatever they used on the floors and walls in the basement helped enormously. My insurance agent came by, took his own photos, and informed me that since the washer and dryer had been second-hand and old, they wouldn't be covering the cost of replacements.

What he estimated would actually be covered wasn't much more than the cost of the cleaning crew. Later that afternoon I was sitting on the front porch steps, holding the insurance paperwork, the bills from the crew, and wondering how in the sweet hell I would ever be able to afford the repairs—let alone the cost of purchasing a new washer and dryer.

"Hey." Duncan came out and sat beside me.

"Remind me why it's not acceptable to hex the insurance adjuster."

He laughed and patted my back. "It's going to be okay."

I handed him the paperwork. "Right now it doesn't feel that way."

He went over the papers. "I can repair the damage in the basement," Duncan offered.

"I'm sure you can, but I really can't afford any more construction work on the bungalow right now." Duncan opened his mouth to speak, but I jumped in before he could say anything. "I'm not taking advantage of our friendship by having you do the work for free."

"We're more than friends," he said softly.

I took his hand, gave it a squeeze. "And that's exactly why, I'm *not* going to do that. If I have to, I'll tear out the old paneling myself, and leave the studs and concrete showing."

Duncan stared at me for a moment. "Okay."

"This really burns my ass," I said, and grimaced when Duncan started to laugh. "Let me rephrase that. I was hoping to put in a new vanity and sink in the upstairs bathroom. I'd been trying to figure out how long it would take me to save up to cover the cost of the installation. If I've learned anything from the reno, nothing with plumbing is ever simple in an older home." I ran a hand through my hair. "Now instead I have to work on the basement."

"Would it make you feel better to get started on the tear-out today?" Duncan asked.

I sighed. "You know me too well."

A Quinn construction truck pulled up to the curb in front of my house. To my surprise, Marshall from Duncan's crew hopped out. He waved at us and went around to the back of the pickup truck.

"Before you yell," Duncan began, "Marshall dropped by to help me haul the washing machine out of the basement."

"I could have helped you," I said.

"Marshall has an appliance dolly. It's quicker and safer to move it that way."

Marshall began wheeling the dolly up the driveway. His long blonde hair was tied back in a ponytail, and his baseball cap had seen better days. "Hey there." He nodded to me all good cheer.

"Hi Marshall. How's Felicia and your daughter?"

"They're doing good. Wife's not feeling too great at

the moment."

"Why? What's wrong?" Duncan asked, sounding concerned.

Marshall stopped at the base of the steps. "Oh nothing that won't sort itself out in a few months. She's pregnant. We're pregnant. Again."

Duncan went bounding down the steps and gave his friend a quick hug. I watched as the two men slapped each other on the back, and laughed.

"When is she due?" I asked.

"April," he answered.

I smiled. "That'd be a great name if you have another girl."

Marshall tipped back his hat and sighed. "That's what the wife thinks."

Marshall and Duncan went right to work. They strapped the washing machine to the appliance dolly and hauled it up the basement steps. I tried not to laugh at the good natured swearing they indulged in while they wrangled it up the stairs and out the kitchen door. Once it was out, they rolled it around and I helped them load it up in the back of the truck. Next, they went for the dryer that was still in the backyard, and added that to the pickup bed.

When Marshall offered to haul away the damaged paneling, I took a pair of work gloves out of the garage, grabbed my hammer and went down to the basement. Together the three of us began pulling it down. It was quick work, as the paneling had simply been tacked to the studs. There hadn't even been any insulation.

"Someone probably did this in the late 1960's maybe 1970's," Marshall told me.

"It's very *Brady Bunch*." I grunted as I pulled a section loose.

"Yeah, baby." Marshall pulled an entire panel down. "This sort of paneling was considered to be pretty groovy back in its day."

We hauled all the paneling out to the truck, and Marshall gave us a wave and headed off to go dispose of the paneling, and also to take the old appliances away to be recycled or sold for scrap metal.

I stopped in the kitchen to wash my hands and went back to the basement to sweep up the concrete floor one last time. Between the clean-up crew and removing the ugly and damaged paneling, the smell of smoke was almost completely gone. Now, I was left with one entire side of the basement that had exposed framing and visible concrete walls. I sighed and checked under the wooden stairs, making sure that I hadn't missed any stray nails. I saw a few stragglers and I stepped under the stairs with the broom to get them, promptly smacking my head on the risers. "Damn it!"

Duncan came down the stairs. "Autumn? What happened?"

I came out with my hand clapped to the top of my head. "I'm fine," I said. "Bumped my head on the stairs, is all."

"Give me the broom." Duncan took it from me and I

went to get the dustpan. "Huh, that's interesting." Duncan's voice sounded from under the stairs.

"What is?" I asked walking over to him.

"The top step, it's built out and enclosed with paneling, but the others are not."

"Why would they do that?" I asked.

"Let's find out." Duncan pulled a hammer out of a loop on his jeans and using the claw he pulled a section of paneling away from the back of the step. "There's something in here."

"Really?" I ducked under the basement steps and stood beside him. As I watched, Duncan reached up and pulled out a metal storage box from inside the small compartment. He handed it to me silently, and we stepped out into the main part of the basement to look at it.

"What in the world was this doing stashed away under the basement stairs?" I wanted to know.

Duncan frowned. "At a guess, I'd say that little niche had been built around the same time the paneling was added to the basement."

"Marshall had said he thought the paneling was added in the late 1960's, or 1970's," I remembered.

"We tear out old paneling all the time." Duncan scratched his chin. "And I'd have to agree with that estimate."

"That means it was done when Irene lived in the bungalow." I considered the metal box a little more carefully. It wasn't overly large, maybe eight by ten inches and four inches deep. I used the bottom of my t-shirt and wiped some of the dust off the lid, and discovered that it had been decorated.

"Is that a painted symbol on the lid?' Duncan asked.

I rotated the box so the image would be right side up. The simple design was of a red dragon sitting on the edge of a white crescent moon. "Duncan," I said cautiously. "This is a combination of both the Bishop family crest, *and* the Drake family crest."

"I've never seen or heard of the family crests being combined before, have you?"

"No." I met his eyes. "I haven't."

CHAPTER EIGHT

We stared at each other silently, for a long moment.

"Let's take this upstairs," Duncan suggested.

I nodded, and Duncan scooped up the last of the nails from the floor, dumping them in a trash bag. I started up to the kitchen and he followed me. I set the box down on the table and while Duncan went outside to dump the garbage from the basement clean-up, I dampened a paper towel at the sink and wiped down the outside of the metal box.

"I have to admit," I said after wiping off my hands. "This makes me a little nervous." I sat at the table and waited for Duncan.

"Maybe it's a time capsule." Duncan finished washing up at the sink and sat beside me. "It's not even locked."

"Well, here goes." I flipped up the clasp and lifted the lid.

Inside the metal box were papers, documents and old photos. The top photo showed two women standing arm in arm. They wore summer dresses, sunglasses and huge smiles. I recognized one of the women in the photo immediately. It was Irene Bishop.

In seconds, that photo changed everything. "Oh my goddess." I flipped the photo over and saw the words, 'Taylor and Irene 1968' had been written in pencil on the back. I turned it back over and took in the details of the snapshot.

"What?" Duncan asked.

I held the photo up for Duncan to see. "The woman on the right? That is Irene Bishop in 1968."

"Wow, she was a stunner."

"That's not what is shocking to me," I said.

Duncan frowned over the photo. "She's on a beach, Florida maybe."

"And she's heavily pregnant!" When Duncan stared at me, I rushed to explain. "According to the family tree and history, Irene Bishop never married and *never* had any children!"

I passed him the picture and gently began to go through the contents of the box. What I found next had me gasping again. "These are adoption papers." I gently unfolded the documents and we studied them together.

"So Irene gave up her child for adoption?" Duncan ran a finger down the page. "Says here that the adoptive parents are Vance and Taylor Sutton."

I grabbed the photo, flipped it over. "Taylor and Irene." I read.

"Which means that Irene knew the couple who

adopted her child," Duncan decided.

I reached in and pulled out another official looking, smaller document. "This is a birth certificate." I began to read. "The baby was a girl. Born August 21, 1968. Six pounds, eleven ounces, twenty inches long." I scanned the parental information next. "Mother: Irene Catherine Bishop."

"Who was the father?" Duncan asked.

I skimmed my finger down the certificate, and what I saw had my jaw dropping. "Father: Phillip Samuel Drake."

"That would have been my great-uncle." Duncan blew out a long breath. "What else is in the box?"

We meticulously went through the rest of the contents. We found a black and white photo of Irene and Phillip together that was dated 1966. I recognized Phillip from the picture Olivia had given me, and the newspaper photo I had found during my internet search.

"Hang on a second. I have an idea!" I dashed upstairs and hauled the bulletin board down with me. "Check this out." I quickly shared with him the other information I'd gathered on my great-aunt, and Silas and Phillip Drake.

We went back to the exploration of the box, and the fragrance of lilacs drifted through the kitchen—which was comforting and sad all at the same time. There was a love letter from Phillip to Irene, and two dozen or so faded color photos of Irene with her little girl. Clearly she had known the child during her lifetime.

We rearranged the pictures by the dates stamped or written on the back, and when all was said and done we had a little timeline of Irene and her child. The girl's name was Patricia, and there were photos of Irene and her daughter up until Patricia was an adult. The most recent photo was dated 1989 and showed Patricia wearing a wedding ring, and a maternity dress.

"When did Irene pass away?" Duncan asked.

I referred to the bulletin board. "She died in 1990. It was after her death that the bungalow was sold to the Greenes."

"That night that Irene spoke through you," Duncan said, studying the photos. "She asked me to help her. To bring back what was secreted away."

Overwhelmed, I sat back in my chair. "So she wants us to find Patricia?" The basement door began to slowly shut on its own.

"And her child." Duncan reminded me.

The scent of lilacs intensified. "I'll take that as a *yes*," I said to the room.

"We may have uncovered the reason the bungalow is haunted," Duncan said thoughtfully.

"Good point. I suppose I should talk to Nathan about all this."

"The haunting?" Duncan rubbed his hand over his chin. "Yes, but maybe you could hold off for a few days about the lock box and its contents."

I raised an eyebrow at him.

"There's legalities to consider," Duncan said. "What

if Patricia doesn't want to be found?"

"Good point." I picked up the last photo. "She appears close to her mother, and yet my own family never knew of her existence."

Duncan tapped on the adoption papers. "Irene had said she was *secreted* away. Maybe there was a reason for that."

"I suppose I could try an internet search." I gazed down at the photo of Irene and her adult daughter. "We have her maiden name and her birth date. Although, that might take some time."

"I have an alternative suggestion," Duncan said. "I know someone who would have the resources to hire someone to do the research and to track them down quickly."

"Who?" I asked.

Duncan's blue eyes were intense. "Thomas."

I nodded. "You're right."

"I'm surprised you agree."

"This isn't only a Bishop family matter," I said. "Patricia and her child are descendants of *both* the Bishop and Drake family lines."

Duncan began to gather up all the photos. "I'll call my uncle and make arrangements for us to see him. Tonight if possible."

I nestled the rest of the papers back in the box. "I think that's wise. I'd like to have as much information as possible before I share this with my family."

***

I wasn't sure if I was excited about or dreading the meeting with Thomas Drake inside of their family mansion. The last time I'd been in the building, I'd fought for my life. *Then again,* I thought glancing over at Duncan as we drove through town, *on that horrible night, so had Duncan.*

I was prepared for our meeting. Having used my printer/ copier, I'd made copies of everything. Taking care of that at home had allowed me enough time to get cleaned up, and I had tucked everything into a large tote bag. I chose my outfit with care, and was wearing my good black dress slacks and a bright purple top. I tossed a pleather jacket over the sleeveless top and zipped up my black, witchy boots.

We'd gone to the *Old World Pub* and sat in a private booth in the corner and made an effort to simply enjoy ourselves. For an hour we put family drama and mystery aside and tried to act like a regular couple on a date.

Now we were pulling into the Drake family estate, and I eased my car around the back and parked off to the side of the large multi-car garage. Taking a deep breath, I psyched myself up and took Duncan's hand.

We crossed the back gardens and the large brick courtyard with ivy growing over the walls. The old massive oak tree that had once stood dying in the center of the courtyard had been removed, and a young ornamental tree was planted in its place. Mounds of purple and white mums were planted at its base. Now, in addition to the flickering gaslight lanterns, decorative solar lighting was also dotted around the courtyard. What had once been foreboding and neglected had been ruthlessly cleaned out and re-designed.

"This is lovely," I said to Duncan.

"We had it redone after the third floor was renovated." Duncan said.

I nodded and felt anxiety churn through my system as we approached the carved door at the rear of the mansion. It had been repainted to a bright cheerful teal. Spiral evergreens were planted in decorative ceramic urns, and they flanked either side of the door. Duncan opened the door for me, and I took a deep breath, tightened my grip on the large tote bag I carried, and stepped inside.

The parquet floor was polished to a high sheen, and the thick heels of my boots made little noise against them. Suddenly glad I'd dressed up, I told myself not to feel intimidated by the sheer size of the home. Duncan reached for my hand again and I took his. I flashed him a smile, put my shoulders back and walked with him.

"Nervous?" Duncan gave my hand a bolstering squeeze.

"*Pfft.*" I rolled my eyes. "Not on your life, Quinn." *And If I was, I'd never admit to it anyway.*

We entered a stunning room with high shelves made from deep, rich wood. The library was impressive and its shelves were completely filled with books. I noted leather bound antiques, paperback novels, hardbacks, and college textbooks. There was even a rolling library ladder on a rail. "Gorgeous," I said under my breath.

A cheerful blaze burned across the room in a rustic stone fireplace, and a couple of leather sofas and chairs were arranged strategically to face it. Sitting in a club chair before the fire, sipping at a snifter of brandy, was Thomas Drake. The older man got to his feet as we entered the room. He was immaculately dressed in a suit that had to be custom made. It fit too well to be anything else.

"Duncan, Autumn, come in."

Duncan walked straight to the older man and to my surprise enveloped him in an affectionate hug. "Thanks for seeing us."

I worked hard not to react to the exchange between the men. "Mr. Drake." I nodded politely.

"Please call me Thomas," he said smoothly.

"Thomas," I managed. While Thomas went through the social niceties of offering us a drink, I checked him out and tried to get a read on him. He was *nervous*, I realized. Which was the last thing I had ever expected —but his nervousness helped abate my own.

He gestured to Duncan and I to take a seat, and Duncan chose a leather couch next to his uncle's chair. I sat beside Duncan and gently placed the tote bag on the coffee table that was in front of us.

Thomas considered the tote bag and then studied our

faces. "What have you brought to me?"

Duncan looked to me, and I nodded. He reached inside the bag and took out the metal box. "We found this today, at Autumn's house."

Duncan opened the box and I picked up the photo of Phillip and Irene. I handed it to him first. "Thomas," I began, "today we discovered that my great-aunt Irene Bishop and your uncle Phillip had a child."

"What?" Thomas' eyes grew large in his face, and he went pale. "That's impossible."

"Uncle," Duncan said. "There is a birth certificate, and photos."

Thomas Drake reacted like he'd been sucker punched. I might not have been an empath like my cousin Holly, but it was clear to see that this revelation was upsetting to the man.

Going on instinct I scooted over to the opposite side of the sofa, and patted the now empty couch cushion between me and Duncan. "Come sit over here, and I'll show you what we found. Maybe you can help us decide what we should do."

"I—" Thomas closed his mouth shook his head and tried again. "Alright." He walked over and sat. Duncan smiled over at me, and together we shared with him the contents of the box.

"So I have a cousin, and she has a child," Thomas said some time later, holding the birth certificate in a trembling hand. "This is amazing."

"How much do you remember about Phillip?"

Duncan asked.

Thomas leaned back against the sofa. "He was kind and soft spoken. Phillip was an English professor at the University, and a Master Mason. He and my father did not get along."

"That would be Silas?" I tried to clarify.

"Yes, he was a hard man. After Phillip passed away, the inheritance fell to my father, Silas." Thomas picked up the photo of a twenty-something Patricia, and the photo of Phillip and Irene. "My cousin resembles her father."

"I leaned over and studied the images for myself. "Yes, she does."

"She's beautiful," Duncan said quietly.

Thomas sighed. "My father was obsessed with the male line of magickal succession within the family. Females were never good enough, in *his* opinion."

"Rebecca said as much, the night we recovered the Blood Moon Grimoire." I cringed hearing my own words. "I'm sorry, Duncan."

"No, don't apologize." Duncan gave me a sad, lopsided smile. "My mother *was* obsessed with power. It took me a long time to work past what she did—to your family, to my father, and to me."

Thomas patted Duncan's shoulder. "You've worked hard, and have made excellent progress with Dr. Basu."

Duncan sighed. "I wasn't happy when you insisted I go to therapy."

My eyes grew wide at the exchange between the two

men. *Duncan had gone to therapy? I'd had no idea.*

Thomas rested his hand on Duncan's arm. "After everything that happened, it was the wisest decision for you, Julian and myself."

"Wait," I interrupted them, "are you telling me that you all did family counseling?"

With care, Thomas replaced the photos and paperwork. "Yes we did. I felt it was for the best."

Duncan's eyes locked onto mine. "It took me a few years worth of counseling to be able to admit that my mother, essentially, violated my will."

I'd never thought about it that way, I thought with a sudden clarity. *The truth of it was she* had *abused Duncan emotionally. Stripping away his free will all in the pursuit of the ultimate magickal power.*

"My father Silas' pursuit of arcane power drove him mad." Thomas took a sip of brandy. "In the end, Rebecca was exactly like him. And her obsession for the grimoire is what ultimately killed her."

Duncan slid an arm around his uncle's shoulders in silent support.

Thomas appeared miserable as he sat there, and my heart ached seeing the two men so unhappy. Determined to lighten the mood, I gave Thomas's knee a bolstering pat. "Come on you guys, don't be so gloomy." When they both blinked in surprise, I smiled. "I seem to recall a smooth and suave magician with salt and pepper hair strolling in, kicking ass, and saving the day."

Duncan started to laugh, and one side of Thomas' mouth kicked up a tiny bit. "Smooth and suave?" Thomas asked, lifting his brows.

"Don't let that go to your head," I suggested.

Thomas almost laughed, but cleared his throat instead. "With your permission, I'd like to have copies made of everything."

I reached into the bag and pulled out a stack of papers. "I had all the paperwork and photos copied, I also scanned them into my computer at home." I handed him a stack. "These copies are for you."

"Thank you." Thomas accepted the papers "For now, may I suggest having the originals put into a—"

"Safety deposit box," I finished for him. "Yes. I'm going to take care of that first thing in the morning." I cleared my throat. "Full disclosure? I haven't told my family about this discovery. Not yet."

"I see," Thomas said gravely.

I shut the lid and closed the latch on the box before I raised my eyes to his. "I felt..." I paused and corrected myself. "Duncan and I felt we should come to you first, and then see what you could find."

Thomas inclined his head. "I'm honored you would trust me to do so."

"After all, Patricia is your family too," I said.

Thomas nodded in approval. "Excellent. I'll contact my attorney and hire a private investigator and get the ball rolling. I'll do whatever I can to find Patricia, and her child."

"Will you please keep me updated on any progress you make?" I asked politely, slipping the box back into the tote bag.

"Of course I will," Thomas said, flipping through the papers I'd made for him.

Duncan stood and held out a hand to me. We said our goodbyes to Thomas, and Duncan escorted me out of the library. We'd gone about twenty feet down the nearest hall before he pulled me in his arms and kissed me.

"You were wonderful back there," he said, and laid another smoldering kiss on me.

When he finally allowed me up for air, I spoke. "I wanted to tell you something." I wrapped my arms around his neck. "I'm proud of you Duncan, and all of the work you've done." I leaned my head against his shoulder.

He held me for a few moments, and I could feel the impact my words had on him by the fine tremors in his arms. "Come with me," Duncan said softly, and tugged me along after him.

I followed him down one hall, up a massive wooden staircase, and down another winding hallway. "Where are we going?" I whispered.

Duncan pulled open a door, beckoned me inside, and I followed him in. I'd barely cleared the door before he locked it behind me.

He clicked on a nearby lamp and I saw a gorgeous room. The walls were painted a muted, warm green, and the bed was made up in a white textured spread with an emerald green plush throw arranged over the foot. Pillows in tones of gray and green were arranged across the wooden headboard. The vibrations announced it to be Duncan's room.

"This is a great space," I said appreciatively. I set the tote bag down and wandered the room. I ran my fingers over a sleek modern nightstand, and noticed that the dresser and headboard were both made from the same pale blonde wood.

Black and white architectural photography was arranged on the walls, and as I took in the room, Duncan walked over and clicked on small lamp that rested on the nightstand. "Do you recognize the photographs?" he asked.

I walked over to the nearest one. "Maybe, this sort of reminds me of the architecture around town, but I can't identify the buildings."

Duncan walked over, put his arms around from behind me, and rested his chin on my shoulder. "No," he breathed in my ear. "Do you recognize the photographer?"

I leaned a bit closer and tried to make out the tiny signature at the bottom of the photo. "These are Ivy's?" I was shocked. "Where did you get them?"

"I bought them when the photography class put on an exhibit last year. I fell for the photos before I recognized that they were hers."

"She never told me," I said.

"She doesn't know."

"They look good in here," I said.

"So do you." Duncan began to nibble on the nape of my neck.

"I'm on to you buddy," I said jokingly as he reached around to my slacks and unzipped them. "You lured me back to your room to see your etchings, so you could try and get in my pants."

Duncan pushed my slacks down, and reached for my panties. "I'm already *in* your pants," he growled in my ear and I shivered. He flexed his fingers and my head fell back against his chest.

"You might..." I gasped, "want to let me take my boots off first."

Duncan moved around to stand in front of me. He bent down and carefully pulled my pant legs over my dress boots. I rested my hand on his back while I lifted one foot and then the other. He took the slacks, shook them out and draped them over a nearby upholstered chair. My heart started to race as he methodically slid my jacket off, folded it and laid it on top my slacks. The purple top went next until I stood before him in my purple bra, black underwear and boots.

Duncan took my hand and led me to his bed. His mood was different. The playful and fun lover I'd known years ago, and the spontaneous and passionate lover I'd recently rediscovered, had stepped aside. The blue-eyed man who focused on me now, had my mouth going dry.

He nudged me back on his bed, and my back hit the plush throw. I lay back and watched him as he stepped out of his shoes, stripped his clothes off, and he never said a word. He leaned over me, reached out and hooked a finger under my black lace underwear, and began to slowly ease them down.

"My boots," I managed to say.

"Leave them." His voice was low and husky and made my insides start to quiver. He took my glasses off my nose and set them on the night stand. Duncan turned to me, looped his hands under my knees and tugged me forward. I slid easily against the plush throw. He stepped between my thighs and stared down at me for a long moment.

"Duncan," I said, wondering what he was waiting for.

"Wrap your legs around me," he whispered.

Fascinated by the different mood and his intensity, I did. I'd barely hooked my ankles when he grabbed my hips and slid forward. I hissed at the penetration, and watched as he threw his head back. The nightstand light flickered. With a low growl, Duncan pulled me closer, and began to thrust.

I bit back a scream and that seemed to spurn him on. Duncan rolled his hips, and every clear thought I had went right out of my mind. I surrendered my control and our magick melded and combined, becoming one.

He took me again and again. In positions we'd never tried before and with an intensity and sensual skill that I was unprepared for. There were no words spoken between us, however I had little doubt as to his passion for me. Afterwards I found myself sprawled naked, face down on his bed. I shook my head to clear it and pushed up to my elbows.

Everything we'd done over the past few hours played back in my mind and I grinned. I rolled over and found that my lover was sound asleep on his back, with his arm flung out to his side.

I squinted in the soft light and eased off the bed. I made my way to the nightstand, found my glasses and slipped them on. The old fashioned wind up clock on his nightstand read 2:00am. While Duncan slept away, I scooped up my clothes, found my boots where Duncan had thrown them at some point, and made my way into his en-suite bathroom.

I closed the door behind me and cleaned up a little, got redressed, picked up my boots and eased back out the door. I smirked when I saw that Duncan was still sound asleep, and apparently oblivious to my movements around the bedroom.

I decided to let him sleep. *After all,* I thought, *he'd certainly earned it.* I really wanted to climb back in that bed and do it all over again...But I needed to get home. I had to go to work in a few hours. Inspired, I pulled a lipstick out of my bag, snuck into his bathroom and left him a sassy little message on the mirror.

I wrote, *Woof!* Added XOXO under it and drew a heart around it all. I almost wished I could be there to see his reaction.

Feeling proud of myself, I tiptoed my way across the room, picked up the tote bag and eased out into the hall. I reversed the route we had taken to get to his room and I managed to navigate my way back out.

I congratulated myself on my success when I silently shut the teal door behind me. I took a few steps forward on the brick pavers and I clapped a hand over my mouth and squelched down a case of nervous giggles.

An owl called from somewhere on the estate and I quickly crossed the courtyard in my bare feet. A bright waning moon ensured that I didn't trip over anything as I moved through the courtyard. I placed my things on the passenger seat, slipped in and started up the car. I backed up and headed for home.

I drove up the hill towards my house, enjoying the starlight and quiet streets. When I pulled in my own driveway, I saw Luna sitting in the living room front window as if she was waiting for me.

My front porch light was burning and I headed up the front steps as Luna scrambled out of the window. Once I let myself inside, I found Luna sitting on the maple interior steps. She let out a loud *meow* as I shut the door behind me.

I flipped the lock and the cat pounced on my feet and gave my toes a good nip. "Ouch!" I jumped back. "Okay, okay. What? Are you starving or something?"

Luna flipped her tail high and sauntered towards the kitchen. Properly chastised, I dropped my boots and the bag on the sectional and walked into the kitchen that was softly lit by the under the counter lighting. I expected to find the cat's food bowl empty, but it was mostly full, as was her water dish.

I glared from the bowls to the cat. "You've got food," I said to Luna. "What was that all about?"

"Maybe she doesn't approve of you being out so late," a female voice said from behind me.

I jumped, spun towards the sound and came face to face with the ghost of Irene Bishop. I couldn't help but squeak a little when I found her leaning against my staircase with her arms folded across her chest.

"Irene!" I slapped a hand to my chest. "What are you doing here?"

"I live here," she reminded me.

I blew out a breath. "Well yes, I'm very aware that you live here. You're not exactly subtle. I *meant,* what are you doing here...because you're looking very corporeal. And damn it woman, you scared me!"

"I'm sorry if I frightened you," Irene said, but the grin on her face made the words less than sincere. Luna scampered across the room and sat next to the ghost, as if she were siding with Irene.

I moved closer to the ghost, wanting to take in the details of her appearance. Irene's dark hair was streaked with silver, and her eyes were a deep blue. Her dress was simple and reminded me of the first time I'd gotten a glimpse of her. "We found your box and the papers," I said. "Duncan and I took the information to Thomas

Drake, he's going to track down Patricia and her child."

"Thank you. I've waited a long time to bring them home." She smiled fully, and I appreciated for the first time how gorgeous the older woman had been.

"Why didn't you raise your own child?" I asked quickly before she disappeared. From my experiences with other family ghosts, I knew she wouldn't be here long. "I saw the photos. You were a part of Patricia's life, so why didn't you raise her here in William's Ford?"

"It wasn't safe," Irene said. Her image wavered and began to fade. As if in sympathy, the cat let out a sad little meow.

"Why?" I asked, but there was no answer. She was gone.

I raced for my bag, hit the notes app and spoke into my phone, noting the date and time. I repeated everything I could remember about what Irene had said, checked what I had down, and added any other detail that I could recall.

I re-read my notes and began to yawn. Fatigue hit me like a truck, and I staggered towards the staircase and made my way to my bedroom. I tossed my jacket on the bench at the foot of my bed, stripped out of my pants and climbed into bed still wearing my purple silky shirt. I placed my phone on the night stand, set my alarm, and tucked my glasses in their case. With a sigh, I pulled the covers up to my chin and was out in seconds.

CHAPTER NINE

I trudged down to the kitchen in the morning wearing my plush robe, with every muscle aching. The sexual Olympics that Duncan and I'd indulged in had left me limping. I took a few acetaminophen, and stared blindly out the kitchen window.

"Jeez," I tried to stretch and winced instead. I typically woke early and cheerful, and anticipating a brisk jog...but today I'd overslept, and the muscles in my legs were screaming. Giving up the idea of a run, I stalked to the new shower and flung myself in.

I stepped out of the stall and reached for a towel, only to realize that all my downstairs towels had been taken to the manor after the fire to be washed. With no other choice, I wrung my hair out as best I could, wrapped myself in my robe and dripped all the way up the stairs.

I got ready for work as quickly as possible, I fixed my face and dried and styled my hair to hang loose around my shoulders. I pulled on a simple, black, knee length dress and tossed a long denim jacket over it. The labradorite pendant Duncan had given me lay shimmering softly against the bodice of the dress. I found my black suede over-the-knee boots. I sat on my bed and zipped them up. The boots had a low, flat heel and were comfortable, plus I was less likely to trip in them.

I fed the cat and was pulling out of the driveway almost on time. Then I remembered Irene's papers and had to stop, pull back in, and run back in the house to retrieve them. I drove to the bank, and it took forever to get a safe deposit box. I was a half hour late to work when all was said and done. I'd finally made it to my desk when my phone chimed, alerting me of an incoming text.

I tapped the screen and saw it was from Duncan.

Why didn't you wake me?

I rolled my eyes and answered with the truth: *Because you were sound asleep.*

I can't believe you snuck out. Where are you now?

At work. I resisted the urge to add: *Duh.*

A few moments went by with no more responses from him, and I started to worry. Was he mad? I was alone in the office so I decided to check in on him using remote viewing. I concentrated on him, and by tapping into my clairvoyance I determined that he was still lying in his bed, with the sheets tangled around his waist. He appeared pissed off and he was scowling at his phone. I allowed myself to slide away from where he was—and focused on coming back to the here and now.

I felt a little thump when I returned, like I'd just landed in my chair. I opened my eyes and considered my phone.

I shot off a quick text: *Quit lazing around in bed and being grumpy! By the way...you may want to check your bathroom mirror.*

Satisfied that I'd taken care of the situation, I flipped my phone over to silent, tucked it in my purse and got to work.

My day was long and filled with one annoyance after another. The printer jammed and I'd managed to fix that myself. Dr. Meyer had lost a file for an upcoming exhibit, and I'd spent an hour tracking it down. I'd eventually resorted to using a locator spell and found all the paperwork in a folder where it had fallen behind the file cabinet. Dr. Meyer didn't trust computers. He preferred physical paperwork to keep track of the items on display. Which is why he was always misplacing his files and papers.

A meeting about the museum expansion ran long, and was filled with pontification from various committee members. The topic of discussion was mostly focused on who'd raised, or donated the most money—more than actual information about the construction progress. I was asked to design yet another pamphlet. Some days I really wished I hadn't mentioned to my boss that graphic design was a hobby.

I managed to get away from my desk at 1:30 and went down to the little café in the museum. They had soup and sandwiches, nothing fancy, but they were expensive. I sucked it up, since I'd forgotten my lunch, and got a cup of soup and half a sandwich to go. I escaped outside, grabbed an empty bench in the shade of a butterscotch-gold maple, and felt like I was living dangerously.

I'd made it through my sandwich and was working on my soup when a shadow fell across me. I glanced up. "Oh, hi Nathan."

"Do you have a minute?" Nathan asked politely.

"Sure." I grinned up at him. "If you don't mind me eating my lunch while we talk."

Nathan sat, and brushed his dark blonde hair back. It was longer than when I first met him, and it brushed his shoulders now. It still surprised me that this earnest young man and my dramatic, gothic cousin were a couple.

"Ivy insisted that I come and talk to you today," he admitted.

"She did?"

Nathan's steel blue eyes slanted to mine. "Ivy had a hunch that something happened at the bungalow last night."

"Damned intuitives," I grumbled.

Nathan leaned forward, and lowered his voice. "She had a precognitive dream about you finding something important, and a teal door."

I tilted my head. "Wow, her dreams are becoming more accurate than ever. But what she saw was more post-cognitive."

"Meaning that it had already happened." Nathan nodded in agreement. "Care to share? I'll keep whatever you tell me in the strictest of confidence."

"Okay," I agreed. "I'd like to get your impressions on the most recent paranormal activity at the bungalow anyway. You'll probably want to take notes."

Nathan pulled a legal pad and pen out of his satchel. "Go ahead," he said once he was ready.

"Yesterday after Duncan and I pulled the damaged paneling out of the basement, we found a little box built into the top of the basement steps. Inside of it we discovered a metal box that held some important family papers..."

I explained to Nathan what we'd found, that we'd gone to Thomas Drake to share the information and see if he could track down Irene's daughter. Then I skipped ahead to the part where I'd come home and found Irene waiting for me.

"Full body apparition?" Nathan interrupted me to clarify.

"Yes."

"And she interacted with you?"

I took a final sip of my water. "Yes she did. I took some notes on my phone last night." I pulled my phone out, tapped on the 'Notes' icon and handed it over to Nathan.

"Why don't you take a screenshot of that and text it to me?" Nathan said.

"Oh sure," I said, and did as he asked. "That's faster."

"And more accurate." Nathan continued to write on the legal pad.

"Now that we've found out about Irene's child, do you suppose the paranormal activities at the bungalow will fade?"

Nathan brushed back his hair. "It's likely, but considering what Ivy has told me about your grandmother's ghost and how she still likes to make her presence known, even after the grimoire was recovered —"

"That the old girl might decide to hang around for a while."

"I'd speculate that she will remain active until her descendants are contacted, maybe even brought back to William's Ford."

I watched a few colorful maple leaves fall and drift to the ground. "You're probably right."

"So you've decided not to share this with the family until the woman's whereabouts can be confirmed?"

"Correct." I gathered up my trash. "Aunt Faye finding out about her sibling's secret child is going to be a pretty big shock for her. It is going to hurt her feelings, and I'd rather minimize that with as much positive information as I can."

"Well, you'd know about that first hand, wouldn't

you?" Ivy's voice came from behind us.

Both Nathan and I both jumped guiltily, and turned simultaneously to find Ivy standing behind our bench.

Nathan sighed. "Hello Ivy."

Wow, epic fail with the psychic abilities, I thought and tried a smile. "Hey Shorty. I didn't know you were back there."

Ivy stomped around the bench to face us both. "I knew, I just *knew* that I needed to come out here this afternoon." She folded her arms over her chest and narrowed her eyes. "Now I know why my intuition has been screaming at me all day that something epic was brewing."

"How much did you hear while you were eavesdropping?" Nathan asked coolly.

Brave boy, was my first thought as I saw Ivy take a deep breath in preparation to yell, or possibly to make him go flying through the air. I held up a hand. "Ivy, stop!"

"You don't get to tell me whether or not I can yell at my boyfriend!" Ivy snapped.

"This isn't helping anything." I set my little cup of soup aside. "Before you shout at me, or decide to blast me all the way to the state line; sit down, shut up and I'll tell you about it."

Ivy sat beside me on the bench. "I heard most of it. Irene had a love child back in the day, and gave her up for adoption. What I can't understand is why you went to the Drakes instead of our family."

"Because the *father* of Irene Bishop's child was Phillip Drake."

Ivy flinched. "Oh, holy shit." She scowled over at Nathan. "I missed that part."

Duncan put his notes away. "That's what happens when you skulk around spying on people."

Beside me, Ivy made a move, and I blocked her from diving after Nathan. "Dude," I said to Nathan. "She'll fry your ass if you keep using that tone."

Nathan chuckled. "She can try."

Ivy glared and raised her hands. "You don't think I will?"

Before she could do anything, I grabbed Ivy's hands and yanked them down. "Do I have to remind you, that we are in public?" I whispered furiously to my cousin.

"No worries." Ivy relaxed and leaned back on the bench. "Nathan and I will settle this later, when we're alone." She batted her eyelashes at him. "Won't we honey?"

"Kids," I said trying to maintain some semblance of control.

"I happen to agree with Autumn," Nathan said, ignoring the threat from Ivy. "The more information you can gather about this woman, *before* you present this to the family, the better."

"Phillip Drake..." Ivy trailed off. "Hey, isn't there a building named after him on campus?"

"Yes." I nodded. "According to Thomas, his uncle Phillip was an English professor here at the University."

Ivy blew out a long breath. "And I suppose old man Drake would have the resources and the money to track someone down."

"This woman is his relative too," I reminded Ivy.

"Yeah, yeah." Ivy rolled her eyes. "But I'm telling you, finding out that the Drake and the Bishop lines have *combined*? That's a little disturbing."

"Why?" Nathan frowned at her.

"Because that means that there's some lady out there with the magick of *both* the Bishops and the Drake families." Ivy shuddered. "That's totally got to be a sign of the apocalypse."

I tried to cover my reaction to my cousin's words. "Now let's not be overly dramatic," I suggested. "When I first moved here Gwen and Bran told me the story about the Colonial era Patience Bishop and James Drake. They were married and had a child."

"Yeah, and he died, and she and the baby disappeared!" Ivy reminded me. "Sounds like history has repeated itself!"

Ivy did have a point. But it made me wonder, *if Duncan and I ever became an official couple...would we face the same sort of derision?* Would our future be as star-crossed as Patience and James, and Irene and Phillip?

***

By the time I got home to the bungalow I was in a

sour mood. With the office politics about the Historical Society, and Professor Meyer being more absent minded than usual, I'd had it. Ivy's words kept circling around in my brain about the Bishops and the Drakes combining. *A sign of the apocalypse...* I took a steadying breath and told myself not to let Ivy's theatrics and my own fears get to me.

I'd stripped off my jacket and draped it over a kitchen chair. I was standing in front of the refrigerator, staring at the contents, and hoping for some inspiration for dinner. Nothing appealed to me. At all. Letting the door swing shut, I considered ordering Chinese food. I was reaching in the kitchen drawer for a menu when I heard the back door open with a solid click.

Duncan let himself right in.

"Well, don't be shy," I said, and cringed internally as I'd sounded bitchy instead of humorous.

"Bad day?" he asked, and shut the door behind him.

"It was a long one." I ran a hand through my hair.

"I thought it would be okay if I dropped by." Duncan stayed where he was. "But after seeing the expression on your face when I let myself in, maybe I should have called first."

"I didn't realize you still had my house key."

Slowly, deliberately, Duncan set the key in the center of the kitchen table. "Consider it returned."

"I don't want to argue with you," I began.

"Then don't."

I studied him as he stood there with his hands tucked

in his jean's pockets and a bland expression. "I was thinking about ordering some Chinese takeout. Do you want something?"

"I wouldn't want to put you out." Duncan's voice had a bit of a snap to it.

I sighed. "We're going to argue anyway, aren't we?"

The black button down shirt he wore made his eyes appear a brighter shade of blue. Those eyes searched mine. "Why did you leave last night?" he asked.

"Technically it was this morning," I reminded him.

"You could have stayed. But instead you snuck out, without waking me, and went home."

"I didn't sneak out." *Ah, yes you did,* my inner monologue argued. I ignored that and focused on Duncan. "Oh for goddess sake. It's not a big deal." Luna galloped into the kitchen full speed. She passed me up and headed straight for Duncan and began rubbing against his ankles.

"At least someone is happy to see me." Duncan bent to pet the cat.

"I *am* happy to see you," I argued. "Duncan, it's been a long-ass day, maybe we could do this argument another time."

He frowned. "Didn't last night mean anything to you?"

"Yeah," I said. "It was great."

To my surprise Duncan seemed to take offense. "Autumn." His tone was censuring.

"I believe I left you a pretty clear note as to my

thoughts on the evening," I said, trying to lighten the mood.

"You left me a note in lipstick on the mirror of my bathroom." Duncan's voice was flat, his expression set. "Like some Sorority girl at a Frat house."

"Hey!" Now, I was getting pissed.

"Are you really going to treat last night like it was a casual hook up?" Duncan asked.

"No," I said, trying to hold back my temper. "Last night was different—sort of a different *tone*, I'd guess you'd say even from when we had sex here a few days ago. It was intense, thrilling, maybe even a little scary...and I loved it." I made a real effort to relax and to smile at him. "Honey, you're not the same lover I knew a couple of years ago."

"It's been almost *four* years since we broke up," Duncan said quietly.

His expression and tone of voice were so serious that it made me uneasy. "What, were you keeping track of the days?" I tried to joke.

Duncan's eyes searching my face. "Do you remember what I said to you three years ago? It was an early October morning. You'd been out jogging. You wore an orange shirt and lime green shorts. You ran into me and knocked me down."

"You got in my way while I was jogging," I countered. "And *you* knocked me down."

One side of his mouth kicked up. "You do remember." He rested his hands on my arms. "What did

I say?" His voice was soft.

I didn't insult him by repeating the casual questions we'd exchanged about my family and his that morning. I took a breath and steadied myself. "You told me you'd be waiting for me."

"And?" He stepped closer.

I cleared my throat. "And, you kissed me."

"I also told you, that I loved you."

I backed up against the refrigerator. "That was a long time ago." My voice sounded raspy to my own ears.

"I love you," Duncan slid his hands up my arms, gently taking my face in his hands. "I've always loved you, Autumn. For me, that's not going to change."

"Maybe we should slow down," I managed. "We only started seeing each other again. It's a little soon to be talking about stuff like that."

"No. I waited for you long enough," he said. "I love you and I wanted you to know."

My heart thundered in my ears. "Don't tell me that," I said a little desperately.

Duncan kissed the corner of my mouth gently. "Why not?"

"Be—because," I stammered. "People that I let into my heart tend to leave, in one way or another."

He kissed my chin, then the opposite side of my mouth. "I'm still here."

"Would you still be with me if there wasn't any magick between the two of us?"

"There are many kinds of magick." Duncan pulled

me into his arms. "Let me show you."

I braced myself, expecting that he would pull out more of the crazy, sexy moves from the night before. But instead he lifted my hand to his mouth and dropped a kiss on the back of my hand. My breath caught in my throat at the romantic gesture. He smiled and took a few steps, gently tugging on my hand for me to follow him.

Duncan led me upstairs and into my bedroom. Once we were there he kissed me again, slowly, softly, until my head began to spin.

When he laid me back on the bed, I shuddered. "Duncan." I reached out for him and he surprised me again, by loving me slowly and gently, while he whispered how much he loved me.

Afterwards we lay in the dark. Duncan had one arm wrapped around my waist and I lay on my back staring at the ceiling. *Holy crap!* I thought, *What do I do now? He loves me, and I'm not even sure I can open up my heart enough to trust someone, ever again.* I checked his expression, and my breath hitched. He appeared to be so happy and content as he nuzzled my shoulder. *I don't want to hurt him.* And that realization had me struggling against tears.

"Don't worry so much." He kissed my shoulder.

"Stay out of my head."

"I am," Duncan said. "But I can feel all the emotions you are trying to suppress."

"I don't know what I'm feeling right now," I admitted.

"What does your heart tell you?" he asked as he ran his hands over my midriff. "What do you see for your own future?"

I caught his hand before it went any lower. If he started that, I'd lose every coherent thought. "I can't see my own future clearly, Duncan," I said. "I've never been able to."

Duncan raised up on an elbow and peered down at me. "You're afraid."

Normally I'd take a swipe at anyone who would have said that, but he was right. I was afraid and I truly didn't want to hurt him. I cleared my throat and tried to be honest. "If I knew what my heart was telling me, I wouldn't be so afraid."

Duncan stared down at me for a long moment. "Okay," he said, and dropped a sweet kiss on my mouth. He eased back. "Let's get something to eat and simply enjoy the evening."

My relief that he was dropping the topic was so huge that it was almost embarrassing. "Okay," I said.

"Why don't I run you a bath, and I'll order us some dinner?"

I sat up slowly. "That'd be nice."

He patted my thigh. "Wait right here," he said, and hopped up to start the water in the bathroom.

I scowled after him and wondered what he was up to.

For the rest of the week Duncan showed up at the bungalow shortly after I arrived home from work. On

Wednesday he brought over a bottle of wine and a couple of sub sandwiches. We'd sat at the little second hand café table and chairs I had on the back porch and ate dinner outside. On Thursday I made meatloaf and mashed potatoes, and he cheerfully offered to clean up since I had cooked dinner. Afterwards he proceeded to show me his appreciation for my meatloaf—a favorite dish of his apparently—by ripping my clothes off, and then in Ivy's words: he yanked my hair back and ravaged me like a lusty pirate.

In the kitchen.

I made a mental note to make meatloaf more often.

On Friday, he swung by, picked me up, and took me out for tacos. When we were done he took me to an art and crafts store and handed me a coupon for forty percent off Halloween décor. I managed to get a few sets of orange lights to trim the bungalow porch, a decorated wreath, some floral picks, and a silk fall garland of leaves—all at a price I could afford.

Duncan bought a life size plastic skeleton and a battery operated grinning foam pumpkin that lit up, and a timer for the outdoor lights while I shopped—belated birthday gifts I was told. Since they were so goofy and fun, I accepted his gifts without an argument.

We went back to the bungalow and decorated the front porch together. The lights went up quickly as the Greenes had left permanent hooks up along the porch from their holiday lights. I plugged the lights in and set them up on the timer for dusk to dawn. I hung the

Halloween wreath on the front door, while Duncan arranged the skeleton on the painted bench. We attached it to the bench with zip ties so it appeared that the skeleton was sitting with his arm draped over the bench.

Afterwards we went inside, and I worked up a seasonal display on my mantle. While Duncan poured us a glass of wine and put a snack together, I moved the family photos to an end table and grouped them all together. I made a base out of the orange garland of fall leaves, and I set the decorative Jack-o'-lantern at the center and turned it on. It flickered away with a realistic glow. I tucked the rustic picks in, and their twiggy sprays and black leaves popped against the rusty orange silk leaves of the garland. Finally, I arranged a few of the mercury glass candle holders at either end of the mantle.

"That looks good," he said, carrying out a plate of sliced apples and cheese. He had a box of crackers tucked under his arm as he stopped to admire it.

"It's not as elaborate as the manor's Halloween mantle display, but it's a start," I said.

"I like those little twig thingies with the black leaves," Duncan said, and set the plate on the ottoman.

"Me too." I smiled over my shoulder at him. "This is the first time I've decorated for a holiday in my very own home."

Duncan held up a glass of wine. "Well then, let's celebrate."

I accepted the wine and went to snuggle on the

sectional with him. We found a classic movie and watched *Hocus Pocus*. Duncan, it ended up, was a bigger fan of old Halloween movies than I was. He spent the night with me on Friday, even though I warned him that Saturday was my yard work day and I'd be up early. He simply told me he'd had a change of clothes in his truck and that he'd be happy to help with the yard.

On Saturday morning I rolled out of bed early, put on my grubby clothes, and he was right behind me. When he offered to cut the grass, I let him, as it wasn't a favorite chore of mine. I tackled the gardens and spent a productive hour pulling weeds, pruning back spent flowers and watering the mums I'd added a few weeks before. The large container at the bottom of my steps was done for the season, so I pulled out the faded flowers and wondered where I could get a big, fat chrysanthemum to fill up that pot. As soon as we were through with the yard work, he nudged me towards his truck, and took me to the McBriar's farm on the outskirts of town.

It was a Halloween fan and fall gardener's dream of a set up. There were hundreds of healthy mums blooming away in a rainbow of colors, bundles of cornstalks, a hay bale maze, scarecrows that talked to the kids, and rides out to the field to pick your own pumpkin. Rustic tables were filled with ornamental corn, gourds, and of course, pumpkins. Pumpkins were everywhere. Whatever size or shape you could want. I saw white, orange, and green pumpkins, warty or smooth, big and small.

I had to suppress a happy squeal. The set-up reminded me of the little Halloween display my father and I would set up every year at his nursery. The place was packed and business was booming.

The prices were fair, but I needed to save up for that new washer and dryer, so I bought only a few mini pumpkins to decorate inside the house, one gorgeous scarlet colored mum with blooms that were starting to open, and two bundles of cornstalks to add to my front yard's decorations. Duncan chose a half dozen nice pumpkins and lined them up on the counter. He also filled up a basket with grapefruit sized and mini decorative pumpkins in white, orange and a striped variety.

"That's a lot of pumpkins there, Quinn." I put my debit card away and accepted my receipt. "You going to talk Thomas into decorating the mansion for Halloween, or something?"

"Maybe," Duncan grinned. "But most of these are for you. For Halloween night and the trick-or-treaters.

"You don't have to do that," I began.

"I know." Duncan grinned at me. "That's what makes it fun."

By the time we were finished I had tucked that red mum into the empty pot at the base of my steps. There were two large pumpkins on my porch and bundles of corn stalks attached to either side of my front door.

Luna sat on my hearth beside the biggest pumpkin that Duncan had bought and sniffed it. A variety of mini pumpkins in white and orange had been added to my mantle in the living room as well, and I stepped back to check the beefed up display.

"Looks good," Duncan said.

"It does." I pressed a hand to my stomach when it began to growl. "What time is it?' I'm starving."

Duncan checked his watch. "It's one o'clock."

I went into the kitchen and checked the contents of the fridge. I smiled. "I could make us some meatloaf sandwiches for lunch."

Duncan's head snapped up.

"Does that sound good?" I asked casually. "I seem to recall you being particularly *enthusiastic* the other day when I served it."

"Are you trying to seduce me with meatloaf?"

"Maybe." I fluttered at him. "Is it working?"

"Woman, make me a sandwich," Duncan said seriously. "And I'll show you some *enthusiasm*."

"Well in that case..." I pulled the covered meatloaf out and set the plate on the counter. "I'll make you two."

CHAPTER TEN

The days of October flew by. Before I knew it we were only a few days away from Halloween—the sabbat of Samhain, and I realized with a start that Duncan and I had been seeing each other for almost three weeks.

He still came over for dinner most nights. Sometimes Duncan spent the night and others he didn't. It came as a shock to me one day to notice some of his clothes were hanging in my closet, and that there was a second toothbrush in my bathroom.

I had only walked in the door from work, barely set my purse on the couch, when there was a knock on my door. *Duncan,* I thought. I stepped up on the landing and eagerly yanked the door open. "Hey there handsome—"

Thomas Drake stood in the dusky light with an envelope in one hand and a pleasant smile on his face. "Autumn."

"Oh, sorry," I said, blinking in surprise at seeing the

elegant man on my front porch. "I thought you were Duncan."

He inclined his silvered head slightly. "I have some information regarding our search. Do you have a moment?"

"Sure," I tugged on the collar of my deep green blouse and stepped back, allowing him to enter the bungalow.

Thomas Drake, my family's one time arch nemesis, bad-ass magician and all around scary powerful dude, stepped down from the landing and into my living room. "Well," he said. "This *is* charming." He walked towards the sectional sofa and took a seat.

I tried not to react to his unexpected compliment or the sincere tone. "Thank you."

"Duncan has been talking about your renovations." Thomas sat back and made himself at home.

I was so not showing him the new bathroom, I thought, and struggled not to laugh nervously. I was saved from making a polite reply as Luna raced into the room and leapt for the top of the ottoman. The cat sat in the middle of it and stared at Thomas. "That's Luna," I said, and took a seat at the opposite end of the sectional.

"This is the poor, scraggly little stray you rescued."

I snapped my head around, even though his tone had been matter-of-fact, the words had me reconsidering him. "Yes, I rescued her."

Thomas studied the cat as she considered him. "She appears very healthy and happy now." He held out his fingers and Luna rubbed against his hand.

"Oh," I said, completely thrown off guard by him as he scratched Luna behind the ears. I made an effort and pulled myself back on track. "You said you had some information?"

Thomas sighed. "Yes, I do and I'm sorry to say that not all of it is happy news."

"Tell me."

He sat back. "We've found Patricia Vance Sutton, she had lived in a small town in Louisiana."

"Had?"

Thomas ran a shaky hand through his salt and pepper hair. "Yes, unfortunately, Patricia passed away last year."

The man was visibly upset, and I didn't think, I simply reacted. I scooted closer to him and laid my hand on top of his, offering comfort. "I'm so sorry, Mr. Drake."

He allowed my touch and studied our hands for a moment. "Thomas," he corrected. "I asked you to call me Thomas."

"Thomas." I cleared my throat. "Were you able to track down any surviving children?"

"Patricia had only one child, a daughter that was born in 1989."

"I see." I slid my hand back to the lap of my own gray slacks. "Were you able to locate her?"

"Yes, her name is Magnolia Parrish, and I have spoken to her on the phone."

Magnolia? I thought. *That's a hell of a name.*

As if he'd heard my inner monologue, Thomas continued. "The young woman goes by Maggie, and she has a four year old daughter, Willow."

"How did she take the news of her birth family searching for her?"

"She was surprised at my call. But fortunately, her mother knew something of her heritage, and had shared that with Maggie."

"That's helpful." I nodded. "Duncan and I figured it was an open adoption since there were all those photos of Patricia and Irene together."

"Agreed." Thomas rubbed a hand over his chin. "Still, I had a feeling. A sort of psychic impression...that Patricia's child needed my help, and I was correct."

My stomach muscles tightened. "Is she okay?"

"Apparently my cousin's death left many medical bills. From what our private investigator found out, Patricia's daughter is recently divorced, selling off her mother's house, and fighting a custody battle, all at the same time." Thomas shook his head. "It's not a coincidence that we happened to locate her now, while she's struggling to keep her child."

His words caused the room to fall away from me and without warning, a vision sprang to life...

A dark haired woman stood on the sidewalk in front of a blue house with a little girl in her arms. She faced off with an angry man, and held her ground. She didn't move at all while the police hauled the rumpled, swearing man away. She looked tough as nails, even while the little one cowered in her arms...

"Autumn," Thomas called my name sharply.

I came back to the here and now. "Sorry, took a little side trip for a moment." I shook my head clear of the clairvoyant vision. I felt my fingers being given a supportive squeeze. He was holding my hand.

"What did you see?" Thomas asked.

I quickly explained what I'd seen. "I'm betting that was Maggie...but you know what? I think I've seen this woman in a vision before. Hard to be sure though."

"Take what you need." He covered my hand with his other.

The contact with Thomas Drake sharpened my focus. As his magick spilled into me, I sucked in a deep breath. My back went straight and with a startling clarity, I remembered the details of the vision I'd had the day that I'd walked past the Drake mansion. "I had a precognitive vision a while ago." I heard myself say. "*That's* where I've seen the woman before."

"Take your time," Thomas said softly.

"I saw a dark haired woman, and a little girl who was wearing white shoes and a blue dress." I bore down, trying to push for details. "The little girl had brown hair and was running up the sidewalk to the stone cottage."

"The cottage on the Drake estate?" Thomas asked.

I nodded. "The magnolia trees were in bloom, and pink tulips were everywhere. The mother had pansy-blue eyes, and she called the little girl, *Sugar pie*. They both had Southern accents."

Thomas let go of my hand, and the influx of his energy stopped immediately. "Impressive."

I took off my glasses and rubbed the bridge of my nose. "Wow, that was intense."

"Do you need anything?" He sounded almost paternal.

"Nope." I slipped my glasses back on.

His brows were lowered and he seemed to be on the verge of leaping to his feet. "Are you absolutely sure?"

I smiled. "I'm fine actually. I feel great."

"You should know that I'm on my way to Louisiana to offer Maggie my assistance."

"Is there anything else I can do?" I asked him. "I mean, Maggie and her daughter are Bishops too."

"Here's her email address." He handed me a thick envelope. "Perhaps you could reach out."

"Alright." I accepted the envelope.

Thomas stood and began making his way to the door. He reached for the handle and paused. "If I may offer some advice. The opportunity for love and acceptance isn't something that presents itself very often. I let it go once, because I was afraid of what others would say, and it's something I regret every day of my life."

"You and Gwen?" I asked.

"Yes, but today I'm speaking of you and my nephew. Duncan loves you."

I felt my cheeks flush red. "He's told me."

"And you? Do you love him in return?" Thomas asked bluntly.

"Well, I—"

"If you are worried about such a thing yourself, about whether or not you'd have the Drake family's approval...let me assure you that you and Duncan have *our* complete support."

I folded my hands, and did my best not to fidget under his intense scrutiny. "I'll keep that in mind."

"Do that." Thomas opened the screen door and raised his hand to someone outside. "Perfect timing," he said. "I'll be in touch as soon as I have more information. I'm headed to the airport now."

"Thank you for dropping by, Thomas," I said, following him out to the porch. I figured he was gesturing to a cab, but instead a huge white delivery truck from the local home improvement store pulled in my driveway.

"Don't argue," Thomas said as the orange outdoor lights clicked on.

I frowned at him, confused. "Don't argue about what?"

"You'll see." He walked casually down the steps, and across the lawn to where his car was parked.

A deliveryman approached me with a clipboard. "Autumn Bishop?"

"Yes?" I asked, feeling like I'd fallen down the rabbit hole.

"We're here to deliver and install your new washer and dryer."

"What?" I could almost feel my eyes bugging out of my head.

The man grinned at me. "You're supposed to open the envelope, Ma'am."

I tore open the envelope and discovered the receipts for a washer and dryer that had been paid in full, appliance warranties, and a business card of Thomas Drake's. On the back was written Maggie Parrish's name, email address, and a brief note from Thomas. It read: *Don't argue. It's a gift, and the very least I can do after what you've done for my family.*

Stunned, I simply stood there as Thomas Drake's car eased away from the curb. He lifted his hand, and then to my complete shock gave the car horn a friendly *beep-beep*.

"He bought me a new washer and dryer," I said slowly. "Oh my god."

"That was nice," the deliveryman replied.

"Yes it was," I answered distractedly. I stared at his car as it cruised down the street. *That was an incredibly generous gesture.* Unsure of what to do, I hesitated while the deliveryman stood there waiting. *To refuse the gift would be ungracious, but I didn't want to be beholden to Thomas Drake. Even though I really needed the appliances...*

"Ma'am?"

I jolted out of my thoughts and considered the man

with the clipboard. Shaking my head at the realization that I had just been politely steamrolled by Thomas Drake, I sighed, and showed the deliveryman the way to the basement.

When Duncan arrived a half hour later, the men were hooking up the new dryer vent hose. I was sitting at the top of the basement steps trying to stay out of the way and reading the information about the new energy efficient appliances. Luna perched beside me, keeping a suspicious eye on the noisy strangers that had invaded her territory.

"Autumn?" Duncan called.

"In the basement!" I called back.

"Hey." He came down the steps, sat on the riser above me. "You decided to get a new washer and dryer?"

I tipped my head back for a kiss. "Your uncle was here," I said wryly.

Duncan lifted his mouth from mine. "Huh?"

I handed him the business card and waited for his reaction. Duncan's whole expression softened when he read the message.

"It was very generous," I admitted.

"Yes it was." Duncan handed me back the card. "I don't think I've ever been more proud of him."

"He totally steamrolled me. In a suave, sneaky sort of way." I sighed. "Not sure how I feel about that."

Duncan chuckled. "So are you two keeping an eye on the installation?"

"I was reading up on the appliances." I waved the paperwork.

Duncan eyeballed them from the steps. "They're very similar to the models you have been considering."

"Yeah." I gave him a bland stare. "I wonder how someone would have known which ones I'd been saving up for?"

Luna abandoned me for her second favorite person and climbed over to Duncan. "Hmmm." Duncan scratched the cat under her chin. "That's so weird. Almost like magick."

I sighed again. "You told him."

"He only wanted to help."

I stood, held out a hand, and waited for him to stand. "Let's figure out what to have for dinner."

We went back upstairs, and I noticed that the cookbook was out of the cupboard and lying open on the counter. "Duncan, did you take the cookbook down?"

"No." He stopped beside me and tipped his head. "It was on the counter when I got here, but not opened. I was going to ask you about it, but got sidetracked with the new appliances."

I eased closer to the book. "*Thankful Turkey Tetrazzini*," I read the title of the recipe.

"Maybe Irene is reminding you to be thankful for the new appliances."

"Oh, come on!" I raised an eyebrow.

"Did you thank my uncle?" Duncan asked.

"I didn't even figure out what was going on until after he'd left."

Duncan crossed his arms. "So, no, you didn't."

"I'll have to thank him when he comes home," I decided. "Maybe I can invite him and Julian over for dinner here at the bungalow or something."

Duncan wrapped his arms around me. "I can help you cook."

"Yeah, that'd be good. I can try out a new recipe." At my words, the cookbook's pages began to flip.

On their own.

Duncan leaned over to read the page. "*Impress Your Guests Lasagna*." He started to chuckle.

I narrowed my eyes at Irene's book. "Lasagna's not a bad idea, but we'll have to dig up something online. I'm certainly not going to use a recipe from that cookbook for a dinner with your family. Goddess only knows what the magickal side effects would be."

While Duncan laughed over Irene's meddling, the delivery men called me down to the basement to demonstrate how the new washer and dryer worked.

***

The morning of Halloween, I tugged on a pair of black skinny jeans, layered a midnight blue vest over a white blouse, and tugged on my over-the-knee black boots. I stood in the upstairs bathroom, while Luna sat on the closed toilet seat, and I worked on applying dramatic black eyeliner and exaggerated charcoal shadow.

"Here's where I try and channel my inner goth-girl," I muttered. I practically had my nose to the mirror as I blended the eye shadow. I'd had quite the internal debate over what sort of costume would be appropriate to wear to work. Finally I'd settled on street clothes that I could morph into a costume and some accessories. I'd ended up buying a costume pirate hat and plastic sword at a Halloween store, and borrowed a burgundy silk scarf from Ivy for a sash, figuring that it would work for a lady pirate costume.

I put my glasses back on, stepped back and checked my reflection. "Well shiver me timbers," I said, impressed that it had turned out so well. Eye shadow colors had to typically be deeper when you wore glasses, and I'd gotten good at that... but this was Halloween, so I went four times darker than I thought I should and hoped for the best.

I grinned at my reflection and wondered what Duncan's reaction would be when he saw me tonight. I tightened the sash at my waist, picked up my hat and sword and clattered down the bungalow steps with Luna hot on my heels.

When I arrived at the museum offices, I found that my co-workers had really gotten into the spirit of things. I grinned when I saw that Olivia was sitting behind her desk, pounding away at the keyboard with a satin, neon green witches hat perched on her head. Her

Halloween sweater was black, orange and green and there was a plastic cauldron on her desk filled with candy.

"Happy Halloween!" Olivia said, waving to me.

"Looking good, Olivia." I winked and managed to catch the candy bar that she tossed my way.

I peeked into Julian's offices and there was Holly sitting behind her desk, wearing a white blouse, a navy tie, and a Hogwarts house cardigan. "Happy Halloween!" I said.

Holly spun in her chair and started to smile. "Ahoy, Lady Pirate!"

I shook my head. "Figures, you'd be a Ravenclaw."

"I like the pirate costume." Holly's eyes twinkled. "I didn't know you were into pirates."

"Sure, what's not to like?" I tucked my tongue in my cheek.

"Ah-ha." She smirked. "You're wearing it for Duncan."

"Stay out of my head, Blondie."

"You're the one projecting her emotions." Holly wrinkled her nose at me.

I was distracted from making a comeback when Julian strode into his office. As usual, he was wearing a gorgeous suit, but today he'd slicked back his hair, was wearing glasses and his white dress shirt was unbuttoned to his waist.

My jaw dropped. The open white shirt framed a royal blue t-shirt, and the large, bright red S was displayed to an impressive advantage across his chest. It was as if he'd been caught ripping the suit aside to morph into the Man of Steel.

"Julian, that's awesome!" I said, and burst into laughter.

He sketched a bow. "Thank you."

"The things you learn about people on Halloween," I said. "I'll see you two later." I gave them a wave and left. It didn't hit me until I'd gone half way down the hall that Holly's reaction to Julian's costume had been a blank face and silence.

I went back to my own office in the archives and thought it over. Julian had always been an attractive man, but the costume he wore today took him to downright *smoking hot*. My cousin's reaction to it had been to go completely still in her chair. She hadn't moved a muscle, or even breathed.

As a matter of fact, the more I thought about it, the more I began to see that she had *worked* at not displaying any emotion. *There was something going on there,* I realized. I'd pushed my way into Holly's mind once, when she'd come home a year ago...and I'd learned more than I'd bargained for. To my knowledge I was still the only one who knew her secret. I sat back at my desk and started working my way through the notes for the upcoming fundraiser, making a mental note to keep a closer eye on Holly.

In the mundane way. By observation, not mental snooping with my witchcraft.

"Autumn, I'm expecting Wyatt Hastings for a meeting in a few minutes, but for the life of me I can't find my notes."

I looked up at Dr. Meyer's voice, focused on the man, and burst out laughing. He stood in the open doorway to his office, wearing steampunk goggles. His hair was spiking out all over his head. He sported a grungy lab coat that had a stick-on name tag that read 'Dr. Frankenstein'.

"Yes, Master." I said, and got up to go help.

"I could get used to that," Dr. Meyer quipped.

"Did you check your desk for the notes?"

"Of course, but they're not there."

"Umm hmm." Odds were the notes were sitting in plain sight—right on his desk—where I'd left them.

"Hastings is a local author and he's actually agreed to attend the fundraiser." Dr. Meyer was rooting through his paperwork making a bigger mess out of his already disordered desk. "I need to make a good impression."

"And yet you chose to come to work dressed as Dr. Frankenstein?" I tipped my head to one side. "I hope your author writes comedy."

"He writes murder mysteries."

"Oh?" I lifted up the notes I'd typed for him the day before. "I'm not familiar with his name."

"He uses a pen name." Dr. Meyer took the papers and began flipping quickly through them. "Now, if you could stall him for a few minutes so I can prepare."

"Sure," I said, closing the door to Dr. Meyer's office on my way out. I'd managed about ten minutes of work before someone cleared their throat.

"Hello?" A quietly attractive man was standing in the doorway of the archives.

"Can I help you?" I asked.

The man was very slim, with brown hair and a neat, short beard. His straight, heavy brows gave him a somber expression, but his dark lashes made his pale eyes stand out. "Is this the archives, or the theater department?" He hovered, unsmiling in the doorway for a moment.

"Yes, this is the archives," I said. "The museum staff decided to dress up today." He continued to stare at me. "You know...for Halloween?" I reminded him.

He startled. "Oh, I completely forgot. Today *is* Halloween, isn't it?"

"*Aye!*" I couldn't help but say in my best pirate voice.

He put his shoulders back, walked forward and stuck out his hand. "Hello, I'm Wyatt Hastings. I have a meeting with Dr. Hal Meyer."

I automatically reached out to shake his hand, and I discerned why he was braced for an introduction. Burn scars spread across the back of his wrist. Thick and red, they disappeared up and under the cuff of his burgundy sweater.

"Nice to meet you," I said, feeling instant sympathy. To my surprise, when our hands touched, my psychic abilities bounced right off him. I almost flinched from the ricocheting sensation, but I caught myself, knowing instinctively that if I would've reacted in *any* way, he would assume that it was because of the scars.

"Charmed," he said, meeting my eyes, almost as if he were daring me to comment.

I released his hand and gave him a courteous smile. "Dr. Meyer tells me you're a mystery writer."

"Yes I am." His gray eyes measured me.

I gestured for him to take a seat. "Dr. Meyer will be out in a few moments." *How intriguing. The man had one very impressive psychic shield.* I thought. *I wonder why he's so guarded?*

"Thank you." He sat rigidly on the edge of his chair. He glanced nervously around the room, and it was clear to see that he wished he were anywhere else.

Determined to make the man smile, I tipped my pirate hat farther back on my head. "Mr. Hastings, I should probably warn you..." I trailed off a little dramatically.

"Yes?" His eyebrows lifted.

"Dr. Meyer is also dressed up for Halloween, so don't be surprised."

He smiled the tiniest bit, but it changed his whole persona. "Dare I ask as what?"

"Dr. Frankenstein," I said, completely straight faced.

A second later when my boss came bursting through his office door, Mr. Hastings had a polite expression in place. They shut themselves in the office for their meeting, and I was surprised to hear what sounded like an animated and pleasant conversation coming from behind the office door a short time later.

***

That night, I made it home right as dusk fell. It was cloudy, with a little breeze and perfect for Halloween night. I let myself in through the kitchen door, set down my plastic sword, stuck a lighter in my pocket, and started hauling the pumpkins I'd carved the night before out to the front porch.

I lined them up so there was a jack-o'-lantern on the end of each step. Pumpkins in place, I stood at the base of the steps and considered my decorations. The orange decorative lights did illuminate the porch nicely, and the cornstalks framed my red front door making it festive and spooky. "Hmm...It still needs something," I muttered.

Inspiration hit and I ducked back inside, snatched up the battery operated pumpkin from the mantle and tucked him next to the skeleton displayed on the porch bench. I clicked the pumpkin on, and the flickering added a bit more flair. It was the perfect finishing touch.

As I stood on my front porch, I waved at Ivy and Nathan as they added carved pumpkins to the display in front of the manor. I didn't have the budget to go all out like the manor did every year for their Halloween display, but I was determined to try and catch some clearance sales after the holiday and see what I could add for next year.

I pushed my tricorn hat back, and got busy lighting the candles inside the jack-o'-lanterns on the steps. Afterwards, I jogged down the sidewalk and all the way out to the street. I twirled back around and took in the bungalow on my home's first Halloween night.

Half a dozen jack-o'-lanterns were lined up like sentries at both ends of the steps. The strands of orange holiday lights added a glow to the yellow paint on the house and a little atmosphere to the covered front porch. The large red mum bloomed away at the end of the steps, and the solar path lighting I'd installed over the summer invited trick-or-treaters to walk up the pathway to the bungalow.

As I stood there admiring the overall effect, Duncan pulled his blue pickup into the driveway. He stopped, and I walked over to him as he idled in the driveway. He leaned out the window and stared.

"Whoa!" He whistled appreciatively as I strolled over.

I flipped my hair over my shoulder. "Happy Halloween."

"I *love* that costume."

"I wore it to work today, I figured it would also be good for trick-or-treaters." I crossed my arms over my chest. "Are you going to pull your truck around back? I wouldn't leave it in the driveway tonight."

He continued to stare.

"Duncan?" I raised an eyebrow at him.

"I brought a bucket of chicken for dinner," he said, as if he suddenly remembered.

"Okay. Sounds good." I fought against a smile as he gave me the once over, again.

"I'll pull around to the garage." He nodded and eased his truck around to the back of the house.

I chuckled to myself over his reaction.

Within a half hour, kids started making their way to the bungalow. The streets were crowded with little ones and their parents, plus packs of younger teens. Duncan helped me haul the little bistro table and chairs around from my back porch so we could sit out front and hand out candy.

I couldn't help but think back to the last time he and I had handed out candy to trick-or-treaters. As if the memories of our first Halloween together had conjured them up, Sophia and Chloe Jacobs came skipping up the path of my front yard.

"Autumn!" they yelled.

I started to grin. Sophia was dressed as Batman, complete with a bat mask, a yellow and black Batman shirt, black tights and a black tutu. Chloe brought up the rear, and she wore a small black mask, a crimson Robin shirt, with a lime colored tutu and deep green tights. The gender-bender costumes were bright, colorful and absolutely adorable.

Nine-year old Sophia had her hair pulled back in a long ponytail, and a bright yellow bow with bats on it completed her outfit. She popped her hands on her hips and struck a pose at the base of my porch steps. Her little sister Chloe had pigtails that were done in little buns on top of her head, decorated with red and lime green curling ribbons.

"Trick-or-treat!" Chloe said.

"Your costumes are amazing!" I came down the steps to give each of the girls a big hug.

As I chatted with the girls, Duncan came down the steps with the bowl of candy.

"Hello," Sophia/ Batman walked right up to him. "I remember you. You're Duncan."

"The last time I saw you two on Halloween, you were dressed like Sleeping Beauty and Cinderella." Duncan dropped a couple of candy bars in the girl's bag.

"We're taller now," Sophia announced.

I gave the girl's ponytail a gentle tug. "And growing up really fast."

Chloe/ Robin stepped forward holding out her bag to Duncan. "Hello, good citizen."

Duncan's lips twitched. "I'm very glad to know that there are a couple of superheroes out tonight." He dropped two candy bars in Chloe's bag. "I feel safer that way."

Chloe continued to hold her bag open expectantly. Duncan hesitated, and the seven year old grinned up at him, batting her eyes. Duncan shook his head ruefully and added more candy bars to her loot.

Sucker, I thought at him, knowing he'd hear me.

I managed to get the girls to pause long enough that I could get a few photos of the three of us with my cell phone. After a parting hug, they were racing down the path to where their father waited on the sidewalk.

"Happy Halloween!" I called to Kyle Jacobs.

Duncan climbed up the steps to the porch. "That kid's superpower is charm."

"Which one?" I asked, following him.

"The one dressed like Robin."

"That's Chloe."

"Those kids are awesome."

I suddenly remembered what he'd said to me four years ago, after I'd first met the girls. "You want a couple of those for yourself?"

He reached out for my hand. "Yes. Whenever you're ready."

My mouth dropped open. My teasing comment had been turned right back around on me, and I wasn't sure how to respond.

"You asked." He pointed out.

I was saved from further reply as I spotted Morgan rushing up to the bungalow. Lexie and Bran were behind him, pushing Belinda in a stroller. Morgan was dressed as Peter Pan and the baby was dressed in a bright emerald sweater, a soft green headband and little felt fairy wings.

I went down the steps to greet them.

"Captain Hook!" Morgan skidded to a stop and

stared at me.

"Tonight I'm a nice Lady Pirate," I said solemnly.

Morgan seemed to think that over and marched past me up the steps and stuck his plastic pumpkin out for Duncan. "Trick-or-treat," he said.

"I have something special for you and your sister," I told Morgan. I went back up to the porch and reached under the table for the gift bags I'd made. The first clear cellophane bag was stuffed with homemade cookies and larger candy bars for Morgan. "Here you go." I dropped the bag into his pumpkin.

"Yes!" Morgan cheered.

"That's a lot of sugar." Bran frowned at me.

I wrinkled my nose at my brother. "Lighten up Bran. It's Halloween after all." The second bag I handed to Lexie had an infant teething ring in it and some bows for Belinda's future hair.

Belinda sat propped up in her stroller and kicked her feet. She let out a little squeal when I bent over and gave her a kiss. "Happy first Halloween, baby."

Bran nodded at Duncan. "I suppose we'll be seeing you at the Masquerade Fund raiser this weekend."

Duncan tucked his hands in his pockets. "Wait till you see the decorations. They've been working on the mansion for a week. It's creepy and somehow elegant all at the same time."

"Oh yeah?" Lexie handed the baby a toy to keep her entertained.

Duncan shifted, blocking Bran's view of his son, as

Morgan sat on the steps and stealthily unwrapped a miniature candy bar. "It's all black and gold with enough Venetian style masks to give you nightmares."

"We're looking forward to it." Bran spotted Morgan with a mouthful of chocolate. "What's the rule Morgan John?"

Lexie chuckled. "Nice try covering for the boy. I'll give you that, Duncan."

Caught, Morgan stood and walked over to his father. "No candy until we get home." He stared at the ground.

"Do I get a hug before you go?" I asked Morgan.

Morgan spun and gave me a hug. Next, he rushed at Duncan and threw his arms around his legs. "Happy Halloween!" he said, and took off at a run across the yard. Bran shouted at him to wait.

Lexie rolled her eyes. "See you Saturday night," she said to us, then she called to Morgan, and the boy stopped at the fence and waited for his father with a sunny smile.

A few moments later the family of four meandered off together onto the next house on the street.

The hours passed quickly. I only had a little candy left over by nine o'clock, and we called it a night. We brought the pumpkins back inside and lined them up on the hearth. I switched off the porch light and locked the front door.

I'd barely made it down the one step from the landing before Duncan pounced. My pirate hat went flying and his hands were all over me.

"Well for goddess sake, Quinn," I laughed when he allowed me up for air.

He cruised his mouth down and over my neck. "I've been waiting to get my hands on you since I pulled in the driveway and I saw you in that costume."

My plastic sword hit the floor as he untied the sash from my waist. "I was hoping you'd like the costume and take the hint." I wiggled my eyebrows at him.

"I'm in the mood to do some ravishing." He unbuttoned my blouse and reached around to unhook my bra.

"Well thank the Samhain gods." I opened his chambray shirt, shoved it off his shoulders and gave his earlobe a nip.

"Be careful." His voice was deep and husky

I unzipped his jeans and did some exploring of my own. "I can take whatever you dish out."

He shuddered, staring down into my eyes. "Is that a challenge?"

I tossed my head. "Yes."

"Take off your boots."

I bent, unzipped the over-the-knee-boots, and kicked them aside. Duncan swooped in and kissed me, and then our clothes went flying.

Duncan backed me towards the rug and nudged me down to lie on the plush gray carpet. I stretched out and sighed at the feeling of the soft carpet against my bare back. He began to kiss me, sliding over and on top. I widened my legs and allowed him to settle closer. He pressed himself against me and I groaned when he tangled his hands in my hair.

"Look at me," he ordered.

My eyes fluttered open and with a jolt I realized that the vision I'd had of us together on the rug before the hearth was playing out in real time. Duncan tightened his grip and it pulled my head back and up. His eyes never left mine as he slipped inside me. He held still for a heartbeat, then two, and finally he began to move.

I wrapped my hands around his biceps and held on. He never broke eye contact as he made love to me. The pace and intensity began to pick up and he caught my hands, stretching my arms up and over my head, holding me gently in place. I strained to reach up and kiss him, but he kept me pinned.

"I love you," he said, finally lowering his mouth to mine, and our kiss went on forever.

Afterwards, Duncan tugged the rust colored throw from the sofa and covered us with it. I lay on my side, with my head tucked on Duncan's chest, and closed my eyes with a contented sigh. Luna came trotting over and climbed up my hip and settled down, happy to snuggle with us while we lay together.

Duncan ran a hand over the cat's head and she began to purr. I smiled to myself, burrowed closer, and decided that Halloween night had turned out even better than I'd foreseen.

CHAPTER ELEVEN

The full moon of November rose in the eastern sky, and Holly, Ivy and I were all getting ready together for the Masquerade Fundraiser. The twins had come over to the bungalow, and it was sort of like old times when we used to live together at the Bishop family manor.

Holly sat on the bench at the foot of my bed in a robe, while Ivy worked the front of her sister's wild curls into a soft twist, securing the sections back with a few sparkly hair pins. Ivy's hair swung rich and brown to brush her collarbones, and was done in her typical long bob. As for me, I'd been a good little soldier and had fought the battle trying to make my straight hair curl. Armed with mousse, hot rollers and extra strength hairspray I'd attempted to do something different.

With the girls help, I now had loose, soft waves flowing over my shoulders. I considered my reflection in the mirror. Now that my hair had grown back out, the waves were nice...I only hoped the style would last through the night.

My makeup wasn't quite as dramatic as I'd done on Halloween, but it was much heavier than I usually wore, and I had to admit that it looked great, even with my glasses. Catching myself primping, I walked away from the mirror and went to sit on the side of the bed. I slowly began pulling on a pair of opaque black tights.

I worked them up and then stood, pulling the tights high enough so the waist band went to the bottom of my bra.

Holly laughed. "What are you doing?"

I gave the tights a final adjustment. "Pulling the tights up high keeps you from having a line at your waist. It gives you a smooth silhouette this way."

Holly rolled her eyes. "You could wear thigh high stockings instead."

I snorted at her. "Who actually wears that kind of stuff?"

In answer, she pulled the bottom of her robe aside and showed off the lacy tops of her sheer, nude thigh-high stockings. "I do."

I raised my eyebrows in surprise. "Whoa, Blondie."

Ivy laughed. "Or you could do like me, and not wear any stockings at all."

"Ah, no thanks," I said, unzipping my cocktail dress from the hanger.

Ivy helped me slip the dress over my hair. I waited for her to zip it up, and went over to the full length mirror on my closet door to straighten the hemline of the sequined dress. The dress was simple, with all over matte, champagne gold sequins. It boasted a deep scoop neck and three quarter length sleeves. It was short, clingy and stopped a few inches above the knees.

Ivy whistled. "I do like the way the black tights contrast against the champagne gold of the dress, Autumn."

I slipped on my black flapper style shoes with their chunky kitten heel. "Witness the miracle of a pair of heels I don't wobble in," I said to the twins, adjusting the shoe's strap.

With a flourish, Ivy stripped off her robe revealing a strapless bra and matching black panties. "I want to know what you two think of my dress." She unzipped a garment bag and I caught a flash of sequins as she casually tossed her club dress over her head. It was all black and gold sequins in a diamond pattern with thin black shoulder straps.

I grinned. "I should have known you'd find a Harley Quinn inspired cocktail dress." I walked over to her. "That's awesome and very edgy for the masquerade."

"I found a black and gold harlequin patterned mask on a stick too." Ivy stepped into a pair of killer black patent leather platform pumps. We were now almost eye to eye. "You can't call me Shorty in these."

I watched her strut around the room. "I don't know how the hell you can walk in those."

"Magick." Ivy tossed me a wink.

"I guess we're three for three on the sequins," Holly said, pulling her dress out of a garment bag. The top of the cocktail dress was solid bright gold sequins. It had a simple round neckline and cap sleeves, and the short skirt was shimmering white tulle. "Zip me up will you?"

She presented her back to me and I pulled the zipper up. "That's pretty, Holly," I said, watching as she went to the mirror and fluffed up the poufy skirt of the dress that ended above the knees.

"Holly, whatever you do," Ivy said, "don't bend over in that dress unless you want everyone to see your thigh high stockings."

Holly laughed. "Here, help me tie the mask on." She held out a small mask in white with gold trim and sparkly scroll work. "I need to have my hands free. I have to work this event."

Holly stepped in front of the mirror again and held the mask in place while Ivy slipped behind her and tied the satin ribbons. I fetched the bobby pins and Ivy pinned the mask in place. With Holly's strawberry blonde curls, the pins disappeared.

"You look like a faery princess," I said to her.

"Or an angel," Ivy said, smoothing a strand of her sister's hair.

I saw the slight reaction Holly had at the word *angel*. Thinking to comfort her, I placed my hand on my cousin's shoulder and got a quick precognitive flash of information.

Holly and a man in a passionate embrace. Green luxuriant foliage surrounded them. It was dark and

213

shadowy but Holly's hair and the white and gold dress stood out. The man was dark. Dark hair, black tux and a simple black mask over his eyes. I didn't recognize him.

Shaken, I blocked my emotions and slid my hand away from her shoulder as casually as possible. I stepped away and picked up my own mask. I studied the champagne gold half-mask with its black trim, sculpted feathers and large gold satin rose on the side. It also was attached to a stick—glasses and tie-on masks really didn't work together.

Holly and Ivy were doing the final check on their lipstick and were chatting happily, which allowed me a moment to consider the vision. My cousin's dress and the man's mask meant that whatever I'd seen would happen *tonight*. I narrowed my eyes at her as she gathered up her coat and purse. To my knowledge, Holly wasn't dating anyone. *So who was he?*

Ivy rooted around in her purse. "Before we go, I have a little something for all of us." She held up three pendants on golden chains.

I focused on the matching pendants. They were little crescent moons. Chunky and thick and covered in tiny black crystals. "Pretty. What are they?"

Ivy handed one to me. "These are black druzy pendants."

I fastened it around my neck, and it stood out nicely against the matte champagne sequins of my dress. Ivy slipped hers on and it sparkled against her skin.

Holly added hers. "Thanks Ivy, these are wonderful."

"Now let's get a few quick pictures." Ivy pulled out her cell phone and we squished together for the obligatory selfie session.

I checked the clock. "It's time to go, ladies." I grabbed my mask and black velvet clutch, and we filed down the stairs of the bungalow.

Upon arriving, we discovered that the Drake mansion had been illuminated with golden yellow spot lights. They'd hired a parking service and as soon as we'd stepped out, a valet handed me a stub and left with the car. I tucked the stub away in my bag and joined my cousins on the sidewalk. Luminaries lined both the front walk and the drive around to the back of the mansion. Men in tuxedos and women in gowns or cocktail dresses glittered and laughed as they arrived to the party.

"Hot damn," Ivy murmured.

Above us the moon shone down in a pale gold, almost as if it had decided to coordinate with the evening's theme. "It's all gorgeous," I agreed, staring up at the refurbished mansion and the rising moon. *Oh god, what was I doing here?* I thought. *This sort of event was so out of my league.*

As if to confirm my thoughts, Ivy pointed out a limo. We watched as a gorgeous couple arrived. "I feel like I've stumbled on a movie set," she said.

I grimaced. "Don't say stumble. Remember I *am* wearing heels."

That made the girls laugh, and suddenly I didn't feel quite so nervous anymore.

"Shall we?" Holly linked her arm through mine.

"Absolutely." I stuck my other elbow out to Ivy and together the three of us strutted up the front walk and into the Drake mansion.

We checked our coats and made our way through the house. We walked past a massive display of black, white and golden pumpkins in the hallway. They were arranged on a long console table at various heights. Some sporting elaborate masks, others were decorated and some were carved. Old gold candleholders flickered away, and I couldn't resist running my fingers along a masked black painted pumpkin as we passed.

To add to the fantasy of the evening, "Hedwig's Theme" was playing as we walked into the ballroom. High top tables covered in black or sequined gold cloths were arranged around the perimeter of the room. Each boasted centerpieces of golden yellow flowers spilling over black glass containers. Tall taper candles flickered everywhere, and on closer inspection I saw that they were LED candles.

I was trying to wrap my head around the sheer cost of the party décor when a hand rested on my shoulder, and a familiar zip of energy ran down my spine.

Hello gorgeous. His voice was clear in mind.

I turned around and smiled at Duncan in his tailored black tuxedo. He wore a golden-beige vest over a white shirt with a matching tie with subtle stripes. "Hello

Duncan," I said.

He leaned forward and brushed a kiss over my cheek, and I was caught off guard by the public display of affection. "You look wonderful." He flashed a smile at Holly and Ivy. "All three of you do."

"You clean up nice, Duncan," Ivy said.

Duncan grinned at her. "I like the dress, Ivy." He focused on Holly. "Holly, the gold and white suits you."

Holly was contemplating the ballroom, and the compliment had her glancing over at him. "Thank you," she said. "I'm supposed to help with the auction tonight, would you know where I could find my boss?"

Duncan raised his hand to someone and I saw that Julian Drake was working his way over to us. He was suave and sophisticated in a midnight colored tux and black bowtie. Beside me, Holly tensed.

"Good evening." Julian nodded to all of us, wearing a plain black mask.

"Julian." Holly's voice sounded normal, but she twisted her hands together nervously.

Maybe she'd had words with Julian over something at work? I considered it, but there was nothing about the two of them—besides Holly's unease—that struck me as odd. "Hi Julian." I went for a polite tone and I pulled it off.

Julian began to talk to Holly about the upcoming auction, and then Nathan arrived in a black suit, wearing a black and gold diamond patterned mask. Ivy leaned over and gave her boyfriend a kiss on the mouth in greeting. He and Ivy wandered over towards the bar, and that left me with Holly, Julian and Duncan.

"If you'll excuse us," Julian said, and he and Holly walked off, talking about the auction.

Feeling suddenly awkward, I tilted my head towards the bar. "Buy a girl a drink?" I said to Duncan, hoping I sounded chic and calm.

Duncan put his hand proprietarily at the small of my back and led me to a high top table near the bar. He left to get us drinks, and I entertained myself by people watching. There were some amazing dresses in dozens of combinations of black and gold. I self consciously tugged my hem down a bit. I hoped my dress was suitable, I'd ordered it online and had snagged a sale.

"You're beautiful, stop worrying." Duncan handed me a glass of white wine.

I focused on him and saw he had a beer in a pilsner. "Thank you." I took a sip of the wine.

Thomas Drake appeared at my elbow, wearing a traditional black tux. "Autumn, Duncan, good evening." He smiled and was so sincere that I had to squelch down my first impulse which was to do a double take at the happy and relaxed expression.

"Duncan told me yesterday that you'd returned to town," I said to him. "How did everything go?"

Like magick, a waiter appeared and set a glass of champagne in front of Thomas. He nodded his thanks to the waiter and took a sip. "It went very well. I was happy to be on hand to offer my assistance."

"So are they both okay?" I asked.

"Yes, they will be. I have retained an attorney for her, and things are moving forward smoothly now. I've invited them to live here in William's Ford."

"In the stone cottage," I said as everything clicked into place.

"Yes." Thomas took a sip. "I expect them after the first of the year."

That didn't give me a lot of time. I'd have to talk to my family and tell them about Irene's daughter and granddaughter as soon as possible. "I have to ask," I said, my voice low. "Does the woman have dark brown hair, and blue eyes?"

"That's correct." Thomas nodded.

"And the little one," I said, remembering the vision. "She has long brown hair in pigtails?"

Thomas toasted me with his glass. "Spot on." He took a step back as if to go.

I touched a hand to his sleeve before he could leave. "I wanted to say thank you for the washer and dryer. It was very generous."

His lips curved up slightly. "It was the least I could do. I'm glad you are happy with them."

"Yes I am. Thank you," I said and let my hand drop.

"I'll leave you two to enjoy your evening." Thomas walked away and went directly to a group of people who'd been waiting for him.

I sighed and took a sip of my wine. "Your uncle? He's nothing like I thought he was."

Duncan took my free hand. "I know. For the past three years, he's been rock solid. Quietly offering his support, and his love."

"I'm so glad that both you and Julian have him to lean on." I swirled the wine in my glass and thought about Thomas Drake flying down to Louisiana to help a relative he'd never met before. "I'm going to take a wild guess and bet he hired the best damn attorney he could for Maggie Parrish."

Duncan slanted his eyes towards me. "Put money on it. He's fierce about protecting his family."

"Who's fierce about family?" A stunning blonde in a gold sheath paired with a black velvet jacket elbowed her way to our table. "Well, besides us." Lexie set her glass of champagne down.

"Hi Lexie," I said, and waved at my brother who was a few steps behind his wife. Bran wore a nice black suit and a multi-colored mask. One side of the mask was black, the other gold, and the center was white with music notes on it. To my surprise I saw that his tie had little decorative masks in metallic gold over the black background. I heroically swallowed back a laugh. "Nice tie, Bran."

"Lexie picked it out." He tugged on it.

Duncan greeted the couple. "Lexie. Hi Bran."

Lexie carried a mask on a stick and placed that on the table next to her glass. "Have to say, as a cop I don't like all these masks."

Bran ran a hand down his wife's back and froze.

"You wore your shoulder holster?" His eyebrows went way up.

Lexie shrugged. "The gun wouldn't fit in my fancy little purse."

Her comment had me choking on my wine.

Lexie thumped me on the back. "So how are you two lovebirds doing?"

I glared at her. "Subtle," I said.

"We're doing fine," Duncan interjected.

Ivy and Nathan joined us. "Hi everyone," Ivy said. "Isn't this nice having the whole squad together?"

"I haven't seen Aunt Faye," Bran commented.

Nathan set his club soda down. "She's dancing with Dr. Meyer."

I checked the dance floor and found my great-aunt. She and my boss were slow dancing out on the dance floor. She had re-worn that black and gold beaded dress she'd worn to the town's Halloween Ball four years ago. "They're good together," I said. "She's happy, and it's wonderful to see."

"Where's Holly?" Ivy wanted to know.

"She's working with Julian," I reminded her. "The auction is starting in a half hour, and they have to get everything ready."

"Oh yeah," Ivy said. "I don't know why they're doing another auction."

"Because the one they did earlier this year was very successful."

A brunette with short dark hair caught my eye.

Leilah Drake Martin sashayed around the room, and she had a tall, buff young man on her arm. She wore a very expensive gown. The floor length, black tulle ball gown was scattered with gold sequins. I knew how much the dress cost, as I'd eyeballed it myself when shopping for the one I was currently wearing.

She spotted Duncan standing with us and hauled the attractive young man over with her. "Well if it isn't my favorite cousin." Leilah pushed her way in the middle of my family, leaned in and planted a kiss on Duncan's cheek.

"Hi Leilah." Duncan smiled politely. "Introduce us to your friend."

"Oh, him?" Her voice was husky and deep. "Who remembers names?"

I recoiled at her casual dismissal, and inspected the blonde man. He had the build of an offensive lineman, or maybe he simply spent a lot of time at the gym. He grinned down at Leilah with a slightly dazed expression, as if he'd had a bit too much to drink.

"Hello," I said, trying to be civil.

The young man opened his mouth to speak, and was ruthlessly cut off by Leilah. "Now, don't strain yourself trying to make conversation, honey." She smiled up at him and pressed her breast against his arm. "You just stand there and be handsome."

"Sure, Leilah," he said.

She patted his cheek. "Remember, I promised that you'd be rewarded if you behaved well this evening."

I felt my stomach churn. *She'd spelled him.* Bran was clearly appalled, Ivy curled her lip in distaste, and Nathan put a restraining hand on Ivy's shoulder.

"Leilah what have you done?" Duncan's voice was soft, but there was an underlying threat to his tone.

Lexie subtly shifted her stance. "Is that young man under the influence of an illegal substance?" My sister-in-law's voice was low and tough as nails.

"No, he's not." Leilah rolled her eyes. "Relax, Officer Butch."

"Leilah!" Duncan gripped her arm. "Apologize now."

Leilah laughed. "Whatever. Can't you people take a joke?"

Lexie crossed her arms. "We'll see how much of a joke it is if he files a complaint that you roofied him."

"It's only a harmless little spell." Leilah made a face. "He's big and strong, it will wear off by morning."

Leilah's name was called by a group of young people, and she sailed off with her victim in tow. She yanked him to the dance floor and they began to dance with her friends.

I touched Duncan's hand to get his attention. "How hard do you suppose it would be to break the spell she has on that poor guy?"

"I was thinking the exact same thing," Duncan admitted.

"I'm in," Lexie announced, making Bran sigh.

Duncan nodded to her. "We should get Julian. He

can keep Leilah busy."

"I bet Holly would be *happy* to help," Ivy said, tongue in cheek.

Bran dropped his hand on Ivy's shoulder. "Good point."

"Let's go," I said, "and find Julian."

Lexie walked to the edge of the ballroom and kept an eye on the couple, while Duncan and I hunted up Julian and Holly. The four of us hatched a quick plan, and Julian went and cut in on Leilah and her date, taking his sister for a formal foxtrot around the dance floor.

I was momentarily distracted at the sight of Julian Drake doing formal ball dance steps, but I shook it off, grabbed the poor lunkhead, and began to steer him off the dance floor. Lexie took his other arm and helped me lead him away to a secluded corridor.

As we walked along, I tried to scan his memories for clues to whatever Leilah had done to him. I picked up his name immediately. He *was* a football player for the University. I received a quick psychic flash of Leilah tucking something into his clothes, and then a swirl of colors and sounds.

Duncan and Holly were waiting for us, and I immediately told them what I had *seen*. "His name is Chris." I steered him to a stop. "I think it's a charm of some kind. In his clothes maybe."

"He's not doing too well." Duncan tried to keep the pale and sweating young man upright. "We need to hurry."

"Let me check." Lexie began patting the student down.

"Look at me, Chris." Holly's voice was soft and coaxing as she made eye contact. "You don't see anyone else, only me."

"Hi, Red." The football player grinned stupidly at Holly.

"You poor schmuck." Holly held her hands out in front of the young man's chest. "Jacket pocket, left side," she told Lexie.

Chris the football player wobbled on his feet a bit, but continued to stare down at my cousin. "Pretty hair," he said, entranced.

"Got it!" Lexie pulled a little bundle out of Chris' jacket pocket. It was a crude stick figure, wrapped in yarn and hair. She handed the effigy to Duncan and he immediately snapped it in half.

Within seconds the young man's eyes began to clear.

Holly dropped her hands. "Do you feel better now?" she asked him gently.

Chris shook his head and reached for Holly. "Where am I?" he asked.

"You're at the Drake mansion for a fundraiser," Duncan said, still helping the young man stay upright.

"I am?" Chris asked, visibly shaken.

Holly gently removed his hand from her shoulder. She gave his fingers a supportive squeeze. "It's alright. You had a headache and we were worried that you were ill."

"I did?" Chris rubbed at his temple. "I'm sorry. I don't even remember how I got here."

"Let me walk you out," Duncan offered.

Lexie took the football player's other arm. "We'll call you a cab and get you back to campus."

Holly and I stood watching them leave. "That little bitch needs to be stopped," she said with almost no vocal inflection.

"Maybe you should let Duncan and Julian take care of the situation with Leilah." I warned her. Holly's sparkly mask combined with the gold and white dress made her seem more like a faerie than a Witch. A vengeful faerie. "You've worked too hard to gain control, Holly, to let Leilah goad you into magickal retaliation."

Holly nodded. "I'll let Julian know everything is taken care of."

"You did good, Blondie," I said as she left.

She tossed a grin over her shoulder. "Thanks. See you later."

Lexie and Duncan put Chris in a cab, and afterwards the three of us went back to the party. While Duncan went to go have a word with Julian, I waited for him at the edge of the dance floor. A slow song was playing, and couples were swaying to the music.

"Hello again, Miss Bishop," said a male voice.

I glanced over and saw Wyatt Hastings, the guest of honor. He was wearing a slick, black suit and it fit his trim body to perfection. "Hello, Mr. Hastings," I said. "Please call me Autumn."

He tugged self consciously on his bow tie. "Nice party, Autumn."

"You sound so grim," I said with a smirk. "You'll have to work on that if you want folks to think you're sincere."

His eyes narrowed. "I'm not comfortable in large crowds."

Wyatt Hastings was handsome in a broody sort of way. He was movie star gorgeous in his slim, tailored suit, but he was almost *too* thin. I had the overwhelming urge to go buy him a milkshake and a cheeseburger—and then stand over him and make sure he ate all of it.

I yanked my snarky thoughts back in line and did my best to be polite to the author. "Well, we appreciate you attending tonight, Mr. Hastings. Your presence here will surely increase the donations for both the museum and the library."

"I'm friends with the Drake family," he explained. "I promised Thomas I'd come, even though large parties aren't really my thing."

"Oh?" I stuck my tongue in my cheek. "I'd have thought the life of an author was one fabulous society soiree and media filled book signing, after the next."

He rolled his eyes. "Hardly. It's more like working twelve hours a day, seven days a week."

"Well, you've gone and shattered my illusions," I said dryly.

"*Sonofabitch*. They found me," he muttered beneath his breath. I blinked at the author for a moment and then followed his gaze. Several women were staring at him. *En masse* they began to descend.

I don't know what possessed me, maybe it was sympathy for the man, maybe it was because I remembered all too well what it was like to be with a person who other people fixated on. But before he could bolt, I took his arm. "You promised me a dance," I said loud enough so that it would carry, and steered us towards the dance floor.

Seeing his chance for escape, he quickly stepped with me. We moved to the center of the dance floor, and I took his hand. I rested my left on his shoulder and he rested his hand on my waist. We began to slow dance, a perfectly polite, societally acceptable dance. The horde of women pouted as one, and moved along.

He stared straight into my eyes. "Thank you, Autumn," he said sincerely. "You're my hero."

"You're welcome, Mr. Hastings."

"Please," he said. "Call me Wyatt."

"Okay, Wyatt." Dancing in his arms, I could feel that although he was thin, he was also solid as a rock. I got a psychic flash of him working out—some type of yoga thing.

"So do you often swoop in and rescue socially inept men from awkward situations?" He raised a single eyebrow and I couldn't help but chuckle.

"Only under the full moon," I countered, and had the

pleasure of watching him laugh. "Maybe you could use that for a character in a book someday."

"There's a thought," he said.

I saw Duncan from across the room. "Tell you what, Wyatt. Why don't you waltz me across the dance floor and over to my date?"

"Who's your date?" he asked.

"Duncan Quinn," I said, tipping my head in his general direction.

"Sure." Wyatt gave my hand a friendly squeeze and we began to dance our way through other couples and across the floor to where Duncan waited.

Wyatt surprised me with releasing my waist and giving me a quick spin. With a bump I ended up right in Duncan's arms. "Well that was slick," I said.

"Thank you." Wyatt gave a gallant bow, then shook hands with Duncan. "Hello Duncan."

"Hi Wyatt." Duncan and he stood there and began to chat.

"So, I take it you two know each other?" I asked.

"Sure," Duncan said, slipping his arm around me. "We've been friends since I redesigned his office for him."

"Your girl rescued me," Wyatt said.

"There were some female fans after him," I said to Duncan. "It wasn't pretty."

"Yeah, well." Wyatt grimaced. "That happens sometimes, especially at functions like this."

"You brave, brave man." Duncan shook his head

ruefully. "We appreciate your sacrifice."

Julian approached us. "Hello Wyatt." He shook his hand. "We're ready for you."

"Of course," Wyatt said to Julian. "Well, if you'll excuse me." He nodded to me and Duncan and followed Julian across the room.

"My turn," Duncan said, and swung me out onto the dance floor.

I wobbled for a second, regained my balance and glared at him. "Please don't try another spin. I don't want to humiliate myself by face planting."

Duncan pulled me close and pressed a kiss to my hair. "I'd never let that happen."

We enjoyed the music for a while, and from over Duncan's shoulder I spotted Violet O'Connell dancing with a very attractive silver-haired man. I had no idea who her partner was, as he, like so many other people, was wearing a mask. But Violet's ombre purple hair was easy to spot.

Tonight, my friend was rocking a one shouldered jumpsuit. It showcased her colorful sleeve of tattoos that ran from her right shoulder and ended above her elbow. The ebony fabric of the outfit was crepe and it featured cropped skinny pants. I admired my friend's style, and decided I'd have given anything to be that assured and casually sexy. After the song was over, Violet said a polite thank you to her dance partner and retreated.

I hailed her as we also began to leave the dance

floor, and she made her way straight to us on very high stiletto heels. "Hello Duncan. Hi Autumn." She winked from behind a sexy, lace covered black mask.

"Hi Violet," Duncan said.

"Who was your dance partner?" I asked as we moved away from the dance floor.

"I don't know." Violet shook her head, causing the golden chandelier earrings she wore to sway.

"Ooh, a mystery man," I teased.

"At least I got a little thrill out of this shin-dig." Violet smirked. "We did all the floral arrangements, and pumpkin displays."

"You did?"

"And they're amazing," Duncan interjected.

"Yeah, I never want to see gold spray paint again," Violet said straight faced.

The comment made me snort with laughter. "Come on girlfriend, we'll buy you a drink." Violet linked her arm with me and we worked our way back to the family.

As we arrived I noticed that now teams of waiters had spread out around the party and were offering hors d'oeuvres and desserts. Also, Candice Jacobs had joined our little group. Her platinum hair was swept up to spill over one shoulder, and made me think of 1950's movie stars. Her chocolate brown eyes were framed by a delicate, laser cut black mask. Her ebony lace dress was retro, with cap sleeves and a tea length skirt, and she stood confidently in the tallest ankle strap shoes that I'd ever seen.

I waved at her. "Hi Candice."

"May I offer you a cookie?" She held the gold tray out, and I saw that there were dozens of sugar cookies cut out in the shapes of masks. The cookies had been decorated in white royal icing and accented beautifully with black and gold piping and edible glitter.

"Oh thanks." I selected a cookie. Duncan and Violet did the same.

"Candice, are you working this event or attending?" Violet asked.

"Both actually." Candice whipped business cards out of her pocket. "Here, pass these out if anyone asks who did the cookies."

"Yes, ma'am." I saluted her with a cookie.

"Gotta run," she said. "No rest for the wicked and all that." She gave me an air kiss, and dashed off to the next group of party goers.

"Did you see her shoes?" Ivy asked with awe.

Duncan tried a cookie, and shut his eyes for a moment. "Did you taste the cookies?"

CHAPTER TWELVE

Around midnight all the party goers began to straggle home. Ivy and Nathan had left together. Lexie, Bran, Aunt Faye and Dr. Meyer went with friends for an after-party at the Dean's home, and I sighed thinking I should probably go find Holly so we could leave.

Instead, I found myself dancing the last dance of the evening with Duncan. He had been attentive and gallant all evening, and it had made me feel a little like Cinderella. Before the clock struck twelve, I was determined to take the last few moments of the night simply for the two of us.

The glittering event was practically over and we were alone in the ballroom, slow dancing, to "Seven Devils" by Florence and the Machine. Perhaps not the most conventional of slow dance music, but somehow it was right—for us. "I love that it's just you and me." I sighed, and rested my head on Duncan's shoulder, enjoying the final moments of our dance.

Duncan pressed his lips to my hair. "Stay," he

whispered.

I'd never stayed the night with him at the Drake mansion before. We both knew it, and the moment stretched out before us. "I was supposed to drive Holly home," I reminded him.

"It's taken care of," he said and brushed his mouth over mine.

My heart sped up a little. I knew he could feel it as we were pressed together. "Alright," I said. "I'd like to stay."

A light came into his eyes. "Go get your things."

I nodded and went to the nearby table to retrieve my mask and clutch bag. While Duncan spoke to the DJ, the clean-up crew started working their way across the room. I took a moment and eased my shoes off, then I glanced over at him, and my breath caught in my throat. He looked so wonderful in his tux. Not to mention hot as hell. *What was it about a man in a tailored suit?*

It struck me again how very different this cultured, high society side of him was, compared to the easy-going, blue-jean wearing hot contractor that I'd fallen for. But as a Drake this type of gathering was a part of his world too. All things considered—I felt like I'd held my own on that upper-class society front tonight. I stood silently, simply enjoying the view. A moment later he caught me staring at him, and I smiled.

His eyes were locked on mine as he walked straight to me. Tucking his arm around my waist, we silently left the ballroom together. We took a left down a hallway and as soon as we were out of sight of any party goers, crew, or staff, Duncan pressed me against a wall and kissed me breathless.

"There's my hot contractor," I gasped when he finally let me up for air. "You've been so gracious and classy all evening that I wondered if I'd still find *my* Duncan in there under that tux."

He growled a little and pressed his hips against mine. "I've been waiting to get my hands on you all night."

"Really?" I ran my hand down the lapel of his jacket. "Because I've been wanting to get *my* hands under this Prince Charming style suit for hours."

"Is that right?" His voice was husky.

I tugged his tie open and unbuttoned his vest, watching as he struggled for control. *Oh my,* I thought. *This was going to be fun.* "Yeah, you've been such a perfect gentleman that it's been making me a little crazy." I started on the buttons of his shirt and he drew in a ragged breath. "Duncan?" I whispered.

"Yeah?" he managed.

"Take me to your room, and don't be a gentleman."

He stared down at me for a few seconds, and then he grabbed my arm and hauled me off with him. "Come with me," he ordered.

Turned on even more by the urgent tone in his voice, I followed happily. We traveled further down a darkened corridor, and I started to wonder exactly where we were going. "This isn't the way to your room," I whispered.

"We're not going to make it."

I shuddered. "We're not?"

He opened a set of doors, yanking me inside and I realized that we were in some sort of conservatory. The warmth of the air, the sound of running water, and the smell of soil and growing plants bombarded my senses. I caught the gleam on the glass from the full moon that played peek-a-boo in the clouds overhead.

Duncan tugged me deeper into the huge room, and I recognized the trickle and splash of a fountain. We went down a few steps and he swooped in and kissed me hard enough that it bent me back over his arm.

One moment it was completely dark, and the next moonlight filtered down from the glass ceiling. Caught up in the magick of the atmosphere, I kissed him back every bit as hard as he was kissing me. His hands were everywhere as he tugged me to sit on a padded chaise lounge. I sank to the cushion, dropping my bag, mask, and shoes softly on the stone floor. I managed to get his shirt unbuttoned the rest of the way, before he turned me in his arms and slowly eased down the zipper at the back of my dress. He'd only begun to kiss the nape of my neck when an unexpected sound had me jumping. I froze and listened, intently.

Duncan stopped too, and pressed his lips to my shoulder. "We're not alone," he whispered in my ear. "Damn it," he groaned softly in frustration.

His warm breath on my bare skin had me shivering,

even as a distinctive sound traveled across the conservatory: the sound of lovers wrapped up in each other. A masculine groan was followed by a feminine gasp of pleasure.

"Who else would be here?" I whispered back to him. Then it hit me. It was probably Julian. It was his home too, after all.

Duncan held a finger to his lips, signaling for silence. I nodded my head in agreement. He eased the zipper at the back of my dress closed, and picked up my shoes and bag from the ground. I felt around for my mask and accepted his hand. We rose to our feet and I followed Duncan's lead. We stealthily made our way around a grouping of padded chairs and a café table. Somehow, I managed not to bump into anything as we traveled farther away from the couple, and out of the conservatory.

My suspicions were confirmed when I caught Julian's voice. Pitched low, his passionate demand of his lover was clearly heard over the fountain's splashing. A break in all the plants allowed for a glimpse of Julian and his lover. He stood behind the woman, pushing her sparkly dress down her arms. His lover's head was tipped back as Julian kissed the nape of her neck and shoulders, and the woman's dress rustled softly to the floor.

The clouds suddenly parted and moonlight illuminated the conservatory. The couple across the room went from shadowy tones of black and white, to bright colors. I saw that the woman was wearing a white and gold sparkling mask. Her hair was wild, curly, and a bright strawberry blonde.

Holly. I sucked in a sharp breath. It felt like I'd been hit in the solar plexus. *Holly and Julian were lovers.* She turned in his arms and kissed him. My vision of my cousin from earlier played out in front of me, and shocked, I looked away.

Duncan quickly led me from the conservatory. He pulled me out into the hall, and began to ease the doors closed.

"Oh god." I chose a direction at random and began to walk as quickly as possible.

Duncan's hand snagged my elbow. "You didn't know they were lovers." It was a statement, not a question.

I shook my head no.

"Come with me," Duncan said taking my hand.

Stunned and unsure of how I felt about what we'd accidentally walked in on, I followed him blindly. In a few minutes we were safely in Duncan's room and the door was locked behind us. He wordlessly set my things down on his dresser. I stood silently as I tried to process what I'd witnessed.

All of the sudden, Holly's reaction to Julian's sexy Halloween costume at work made sense. *They were a couple, and she'd been struggling to mask her emotions and to keep their relationship a secret.* "Well, now I understand why my cousin acted so nervous tonight." I blew out a long breath.

He ran a hand down my back. "Do you want to talk about it?"

I walked over and sat on the edge of his bed. "How long have you known that Holly and Julian were lovers?"

"For a while." He slipped off the loosened tie and placed it on his dresser. "I saw them leaving the mansion one night."

"How long ago was that?" I asked.

"In the spring." He shrugged out of his jacket.

So they'd been together for at least six months. I blew out a breath. "I don't know what to think." My mind bounced around as I thought it over. "Holly is an adult. It's honestly none of my business who she's romantically involved with.

"You're hurt by the secret though," Duncan said, unbuckling his belt.

"I hate..." I was having a hard time following the conversation as Duncan slid the belt free of his slacks. "Secrets," I managed to finish my sentence.

Duncan walked over to stand in front of me. His shirt and vest were open, framing his chest, and he smiled down in my face. "Are you okay?"

And just like that...nothing else mattered. I ran my hands over his chest appreciatively. "Well, hello Prince Charming." I grinned up at him.

A faint blush stole across his cheeks at the compliment.

"Aw, you're blushing!" I said and ran my hands

around to his butt.

Duncan scowled. "I am *not* blushing."

"Yes you are...it's cute on you." I slid my hands up and took a firm hold of the front of his shirt. I tugged him down to me and planted a kiss on his mouth.

Duncan raised his head. "Do you still want to stay the night? If you'd rather not—"

This wasn't the time for discussing my cousin and her affairs. I had a gorgeous, half dressed man in my arms...and I knew just what to do with him. "A gentleman would shut up and kiss me," I suggested.

His mouth hovered right above mine. "Did you want me to be a gentleman?"

"Hell no," I said, and pulled him down to the bed.

***

In the morning I found myself being walked to my car by Duncan. It was early, the sun had barely broken the horizon and clouds were rolling in. We planned to meet at the bungalow and then to go to the manor together, as we'd been invited for lunch. After Thomas' news we had decided to fill the family in on what we'd learned about Irene and her descendants, immediately. We lingered over a kiss goodbye, and I drove back to the bungalow, deciding to get a jog in while the weather held.

I dug out my black jogging pants, a purple top and a fleece jacket. I secured my hair into a ponytail, laced up my shoes and was jogging down towards the riverfront within fifteen minutes of returning home. There was a nip to the air this morning, and most of the leaves had fallen from the trees. The wheel of the year was rolling towards winter, and I breathed in the November air, cranked up the volume on my iPod, and enjoyed the morning.

I was on the trip home when I suddenly remembered a dream that I'd had the night before...

Satin multi-colored ribbons fluttered in the breeze. They were tied to the back of a white wooden chair. The rainbow of colors shimmered prettily in pale pink, butter yellow, mint green, sky blue and lavender. The perspective of the dream shifted and I saw massive white tents. In the dream I walked forward across emerald green grass, and saw pretty white tables decorated with blue glass jars that held a variety of flowers in a happy mixture of sherbet colors.

I was so entranced by the recollection of the dream that I had slowed down. I pulled myself back to the present, shook off the images, and found that I was now jogging past the row of shops on Main Street. Out of the corner of my eye I caught movement and had to make a quick jump to the side.

"Sorry!" I said, almost colliding with Violet O'Connell.

"Aack!" Violet balanced the open box she was carrying and grabbed ahold of one of my arms. She teetered on her heels, but still managed to keep me from smacking into anything, or from spilling the box's contents.

I made a grab for the other side of the box, and we spun around together and began to laugh.

"What are you doing at the shop this early?" I panted, and pulled my ear buds out.

"We have a wedding this morning." Violet tossed her head, and her long blonde and purple ponytail flipped over her shoulder.

I checked the box. "I didn't mess any of the flowers up, did I?"

Violet peered down. "No, all the boutonnieres and corsages are fine."

I stepped back and bent over at the waist. "Sorry. Again."

"It's all good." Violet walked past me and loaded the box into the floral van parked in front of the shop. "Why are you out and about? I'd have thought you'd be all cozied up with Duncan after last night."

I stayed where I was for a moment and caught my breath. It wasn't a secret that Duncan and I had been seeing each other, but her comment caught me off guard. Violet slid the door shut on the van and started back inside for her next load of flowers.

She held the shop door open. "Want to come in? I'll get you some water."

"Sure," I said and ducked inside the flower shop. As usual it smelled incredible from the fresh roses, lilies and spicy mums.

Violet went over to the back wall, opened a small mini fridge and pulled out a bottle of water. "I'd toss it, but with your lack of coordination, you'd break something trying to catch it." She very deliberately handed me the bottle.

"I'd be offended if that weren't true." I remembered to shut off my iPod and leaned against the brick wall of the shop, waiting for my breathing to even out.

Violet reached into her display cooler and pulled out two big fall arrangements. "Be right back," she said, and carried those out the door.

I peeked into the box on the work station beside me. It held a bridal bouquet and a couple of smaller bridesmaids' bouquets. "Wow," I whispered in appreciation. The bouquets featured vibrant fall colors; reddish-orange roses, yellow button mums, pumpkin colored calla lilies, and greenery. The bride's bouquet was larger, and was differentiated from the bridesmaids' bouquets by a trio of large, English style roses in shades of ivory that were worked in along with the same roses, lilies and mums. Teal and orange satin ribbons dripped from all three of the bouquets.

"These are gorgeous," I said as soon as Violet came back inside.

She reached for the bouquet box. "Thanks."

"I really like all the bright colors. I never did understand why a bride would want all white flowers."

Violet hefted the box. "Depends on the bride, and her color scheme. We did a black, white and gold wedding last week. The bridesmaids' flowers were all white with gold metallic ribbon, and the bride's bouquet was done in shades of peach and champagne colored roses. Everyone wore black, the bridesmaids, the groomsmen and the groom too. The only 'color' was the bride—she wore a nude-champagne colored gown, and it was stunning."

"Huh." I opened the water bottle. "I wouldn't have thought about that, but I can almost see it."

"Trust me," Violet said. "I did the flowers myself. They were amazing." She went out again and loaded up the box. I heard her lock the van and she came back in the shop, closing the door behind her. She stood smiling at me, all professional in dark slacks, dress boots, a crisp white blouse and amethyst colored blazer—her purple hair not withstanding.

"So what's the color scheme for *this* wedding?" I asked.

"Deep teal bridesmaid dresses, with orange flowers." Violet said.

"That sounds sharp."

"The bride wanted fall colors."

"What color is the bride's gown and the guys' tuxes?" I tried to imagine it.

"Ivory bridal gown, and black tuxes." Violet waited a beat. "Do you have weddings on the brain, girlfriend?"

"What?" I almost dropped the bottle of water. "No," I tried to laugh, and it came out sounding all strangled.

"I've seen that dreamy look before." Violet smirked.

I sipped at my water. "There's nothing to see here. I think all of the fumes from painting those pumpkins gold for the masquerade has warped your brain."

"I've never seen you as happy as you've been these past few months. Being in love agrees with you." Violet's soft words made an impact square in the middle of my chest.

I opened my mouth, and no words came out.

"And you just turned white as a ghost." Violet marched over, and tugged me over to sit in a chair.

I sputtered. "I didn't say I was in love."

Violet knelt down in front of me. "Sweetie, you didn't have to."

"But I don't want to be in love." I heard myself say.

She patted my hand. "You keep telling yourself that."

"I'm not sure when it even happened..."

"That sneaky bastard," Violet said mildly.

I snorted out a laugh at her dry comment. "I'm in love with Duncan Quinn." I swallowed past a huge lump in my throat. "Again."

"And you're probably the last one to know it."

I met my friend's eyes. "I'm scared," I admitted.

"Scared because you are about to take a chance on him again, or frightened that you don't have the courage to go after what you want, and to be happy?"

I scowled at her.

"Listen to me." Violet took my hands. "Love makes

fools of us all."

"Are you quoting Shakespeare?"

Violet's lips curved up into a sad smile. "Years ago, I was in love," she told me. "It was stormy, intense and crazy. He was older than me, and we were polar opposites—and I was way too immature to handle the feelings that we had for each other."

"Wow," I managed.

"We'd have crazy fights, and the harder we fought...the more it only fueled the fire. I loved Matthew Bell so much that I remember thinking that if I didn't have him in my life, I'd simply die. He was an obsession."

I sat and listened to her. My friend had always projected this calm and confident air, but the desperate and emotionally needy person she was talking about was a stranger to me. "Violet, you're a strong, confident woman, and *nothing* like that person you are describing," I said, firmly.

"I fought hard to become a different woman," Violet admitted. "But back then I was young and stupid, and he was my first love. I shared everything with Matthew, and trusted him implicitly. I went and got this huge tattoo of his name down my arm, and to my surprise it infuriated him." She drew a finger down her right arm indicating where she'd had his name inked. "He didn't think it was appropriate."

"You have that colorful sleeve of floral tattoos on your arm now," I said. "A cover up job?"

"Exactly," Violet agreed.

"What happened? Why did you break up?"

"We'd broke up a lot back in those days. Together again, and then off. No more than a few weeks at a time, but the tattoo had infuriated him and that time we were apart for months. Eventually we reconciled, and things were better than they'd ever been. I was determined to be everything he ever wanted, and I went back to school to try and get my Bachelor's degree." Violet took a steadying breath. "Matthew had landed his first teaching job, and we had this tiny little apartment. We talked about getting married, finding a house in the 'burbs with a picket fence and maybe having a couple of kids someday..." She cleared her throat. "Things were perfect, almost like a dream, and one day he came home and told me that while we'd been apart he'd gotten another woman pregnant."

"What did you do?"

"Nothing," Violet said. "I got up and packed my bags. He asked me to stay, swore that he loved me. He still wanted to get married, and insisted that this didn't change anything between us."

"But of course it did."

"It broke my heart. But I didn't scream, I didn't fight with him, or hex his cheating ass to the state line."

"Please tell me that you seriously considered it," I said.

Violet laughed. "Of course I considered it. I was so jealous that he'd slept with another woman while we'd been apart. But instead, I walked out that apartment door with my two suitcases and never looked back. I heard he married her a few months later. She was some little society type and her father managed to get him a position teaching out of state at a major university."

"And now?" I asked her.

"I never saw him again. And you know what? Not a week goes by that I'm not making flowers for some bride and wondering...What if I would have stayed? What if I would have taken the chance, set my fear and pride aside, and stood by him through it all?"

"I'm sorry, Violet."

"Do you understand why I'm telling you all of this?" She crouched down so we were eye to eye. "I was so afraid Autumn, that it paralyzed me. All I could worry about was: What would my mother think of me, marrying an older man who'd gotten another woman pregnant? What would the family say? Could I ever trust him again? I let fear and my pride win and I walked away from the most passionate man and amazing love I've ever known." She blew out a breath. "After seven years, no one else has even come close."

I started to pull her in for a hug, and she stopped me.

"You're all sweaty," Violet reminded me with a half-laugh.

"Oh, sorry." I squeezed her shoulder instead.

"Don't be a fool, my friend," Violet said. "Love is a spell of the heart that isn't offered to everyone, especially not twice. If you're lucky enough to find someone you love, and who loves you in return, go after that dream."

There wasn't much time for our talk to continue. Violet had to leave quickly to go deliver the flowers for the wedding. I promised to call her later, and I walked the short distance back home in the light mist that had begun to fall.

I was so busy thinking over everything that she'd said that it startled me when I found I was walking past the Drake mansion. I stopped and stood in the spot where I'd first run into Duncan, and remembered.

The Bishops and the Drakes had a long and intense history, there was no denying it. Starting back in Colonial times, with the star-crossed couple whose love had begun the feud. Then there'd been Phillip and Irene in the 1960's, and twenty some odd years later Aunt Gwen and Thomas Drake had been in love, at least for a time. The truth was that none of those relationships had ended happily.

Now today Holly and Julian were secretly together, and I'd been stalling about my feelings for Duncan. Maybe it was time to take a stand and thumb my nose at the sad history of our families. I refused to believe that my relationship was doomed simply because others had been. It was a new century, and we were different people. It didn't have to be all dramatic or complicated...

I loved Duncan Drake Quinn. It was that damn simple and that damn scary all at the same time.

A half hearted roll of thunder jerked me out of my brooding. While I'd stood there staring at the mansion, the mist had become a light rain. I shook myself off and began to walk faster, eventually breaking into a jog, making my way back to the bungalow.

I let myself in the back door and dripped my way to the downstairs shower. Luna followed me in and sat watching as I stripped out of my damp running gear. "I'm going to get cleaned up, and prepare for the family meeting," I told her. Luna hopped up on the closed toilet seat and meowed in agreement. "It's time to tell them everything I know." I patted the cat's head. "And it's time for the truth to finally be out in the open."

I was drying my hair after my shower, and was focusing on the images from my pretty pastel dream. Anything to keep my mind off the confrontation that was shortly to occur. I turned off the hair dryer and decided that I needed to stop stalling. About everything. "Suck it up Buttercup," I told my own reflection. I put the hairdryer away in the cabinet and began to wonder when would be the perfect time to tell Duncan that I loved him...

"Sooner than later," I said, and then Luna gave my hip a playful swat. "Do you agree, Miss Luna?"

Luna hopped down and took off. I chuckled after her and gathered up my gear and walked out of the bathroom wrapped in a large pink bath towel. I was tossing my clothes in the hamper on the upper landing of the basement steps when I caught movement out of the corner of my eye.

"Shit!" I jumped, and made a grab for the towel as it began to slip. There stood my great-aunt Irene, her arms crossed, leaning against my kitchen table, and she was very corporeal.

"You have a glass backdoor and you walk around in a towel?" She raised her brows in disapproval.

"I'm covered," I said tucking the towel tighter around myself. "Mostly."

Irene shook her head. "Do you have news for me?"

"Come with me." I motioned her to follow, and as I expected, Irene was waiting when I walked into my room. "Thomas found Magnolia—Maggie."

Irene settled on the bench at the foot of my bed. "Are she and my great-grandchild safe?"

"Yes, they are now," I said, and relayed the information Thomas had given me. "She and her daughter will be moving to William's Ford after the first of the year."

Irene smiled. "Thank you."

"Of course." I shrugged my robe on, belted it and let the towel drop from underneath. "I should tell you that I'm headed over to the manor in a little while to tell the family about the lock box, your daughter Patricia, and everything we've found."

Irene's image wavered for a moment. "I see."

"Do you have any messages you'd like me to pass along to your sister?"

"Ask Faye to give my amethyst crescent brooch to

my granddaughter. It's hers by right."

"Alright." I reached in a drawer for my clothes. "Anything else?"

Irene shook her head. "No, Faye is much too stubborn. She held a grudge against me for most of my life. She won't want to hear from me."

"I think..." I shook my head as her image faded. "She's not the only one who is stubborn."

"Speaking of stubborn." Her voice floated through the air. "It's way past time that you told that young man you love him."

"I will."

"When?" she wanted to know, and was gone.

"Tonight," I decided, pressing a hand to my belly as my stomach began to jump.

CHAPTER THIRTEEN

Duncan and I arrived at the manor for lunch, and I brought along the copies of everything we'd found in the metal box. I was doing my best to block any of my emotions from Duncan. I had even gone as far as to carry fluorite crystals in my pocket to further help protect my thoughts.

I tried to be nonchalant as I carried the tote bag into the manor house, but of course I tripped over the damn rug in the foyer. Duncan saved me with a quick grab and I managed not to fall.

Ivy smirked at me. "Rug jumped up and grabbed you, eh?"

"Bite me," I snapped nervously.

Ivy ran a hand down my arm. "Hey," she said. "It's okay. Nathan and I have got your back."

I'd called ahead and had given Ivy and Nathan a head's up so they knew that I would be sharing the news with the family, today. "I figured the best time to tell everyone would be after lunch," I confided.

Ivy brushed at her hair. "Yeah, lull them into complacency with a nice meal then drop the bomb—so to speak."

Nathan rolled his eyes at Ivy. "That sort of snarky comment is not helping your cousin at the moment."

"I'm okay," I said, and Nathan gave my arm a pat of encouragement.

Duncan stayed by my side while I hung the bag on the back of my dining room chair and attempted to act natural—but I was a nervous wreck. I found I didn't have much of an appetite, and I pushed the ham and scalloped potatoes around on my plate, doing my best to make casual conversation with Holly who was seated to my left.

Finally the table was cleared, and I couldn't stand it any longer. "Before we dive into dessert," I said. "Duncan and I have something we'd like to share with the fam—"

"Are you engaged?" Aunt Faye asked before I could finish my sentence.

"What?" I flinched, hard in reaction to the question. "No Aunt Faye, we're not engaged."

Duncan gave my leg a bolstering pat, and I reached for Duncan's hand under the table, and gave his fingers a squeeze.

"Is this about the haunting at your house?" Holly asked.

Aunt Faye's head snapped around. "You've all been making jokes about Irene haunting the bungalow for months. It's time to stop that."

"It's not a joke," Ivy said. "Autumn *has* interacted with Irene, several times. I've been there and smelled the lilacs, and I know Holly has too."

"Yes, I have," Holly said.

Nathan leaned forward. "From what Autumn and Duncan have described, we are speaking about an intelligent style haunting."

"Hogwash!" Aunt Faye harrumphed in her chair.

"It's not uncommon in hauntings that the spirit of the deceased lingers if they feel they have unfinished business," Nathan said, giving me the perfect opening.

"Speaking of unfinished business..." I tried to get the conversation back on track.

Aunt Faye scowled at Nathan. "That's ridiculous."

"Morgan talks to Irene," Lexie said firmly, "*and* he can see her."

Morgan kicked his feet in his booster chair. "Reen smiles. She's my friend."

"You've never told me that before." Aunt Faye frowned at Morgan and Lexie.

Bran slid his hand over Morgan's red curls. "We didn't want to upset you, Aunt Faye."

Duncan addressed my great-aunt. "Irene's ghost has interacted with me as well, and she spoke through Autumn one night."

"What?" Aunt Faye demanded. "That's serious, someone should have told me!"

"It only happened once." I tried to calm her down,

and found that I was faced with disapproving stares from the rest of the family.

"When she spoke to me through Autumn," Duncan said calmly, "she asked me to help 'bring back what was secreted away'."

"At the time, we weren't sure what that meant," I said. "But the day after the fire when we were cleaning up, Duncan found a little niche built under the stairs in the basement." I reached for the bag behind me and pulled it into my lap.

Duncan picked up the story. "Irene had secreted away a strong box."

"Inside of the box there were old photos, and important papers." My hands were shaking, but I pulled the papers from the bag and set them on the table. "These are the copies of the documents."

"What sort of documents?" Bran wanted to know.

I cleared my throat. "We discovered that Irene Bishop had given birth to a daughter in 1968, and gave her up for adoption."

"Impossible." Aunt Faye scoffed.

I passed down the photocopy of the first snapshot of Irene when she was heavily pregnant. "No, not impossible," I said. "Only secret."

Aunt Faye was pale but she held her hand out for the photo. "Oh, Irene," she whispered as she studied the image.

"These are copies of her old love letters, the birth certificate, adoption papers and about a dozen photos."

My stomach tied itself into knots as I tried to figure out the best way to deliver the rest of the news. Once it was shared there was no going back.

"For goddess' sake. Tell them, Autumn," Ivy said. "Before you give yourself an ulcer."

"Wait." Holly glared at her twin. "You know about this? How come Ivy knows?"

"Because I had consulted with Nathan," I explained to Holly. "I was trying to confirm if Irene's haunting of the bungalow was because of the contents of the strongbox."

Ivy shrugged. "I happened to be on hand to overhear their conversation."

Bran was studying the photo of Irene. "Why would Irene give up her child for adoption?"

"We learned that she did it to keep her daughter safe," I said.

Holly's eyes were round. "Safe? Safe from what?"

"From the father's family," I answered, passing the copy of the birth certificate down the table.

"Who was the father?" Bran and Faye asked together.

Duncan rested his shoulder against mine. "The father of Irene Bishop's child was my great uncle, Phillip Drake."

Around the table there was a variety of reactions.

Aunt Faye studied the birth certificate. "I remember the summer that Irene went away to stay with her friends in Florida. We didn't hear from her for months..." Aunt Faye's voice broke and she handed the document to Bran and Lexie. "After Phillip's death she must have thought this was her best way of protecting their child from Silas." Aunt Faye's face was grim. "Silas Drake was an evil man."

"According to what my uncle told me, you're dead on with your description of him." Duncan's voice sounded casual but I could feel that his thigh muscles were coiled tight.

"Are you okay?" I asked him. *They were speaking about his grandfather, after all.*

He nodded. "After Autumn and I read through the papers we decided together to take them to Thomas. He has the resources and the money to hire detectives and to try and find Irene's and Phillip's daughter."

"And did he?" Lexie wanted to know.

"He did." I took a deep breath, and told my family everything I knew about the late Patricia Vance Sutton, and her surviving daughter and granddaughter.

Holly sat silently and listened intently to the discussion—now that I knew about her and Julian, I understood why she was so interested. Ivy took a very practical view on the topic. Nathan, with his expertise on hauntings, had several theories why Irene had been so active at the bungalow, and why she'd stepped up her appearances after the box had been located. I shared with the family my most recent interaction with Irene, and passed along the request that Aunt Faye pass the amethyst crescent pin down to Maggie.

The request to have the brooch returned upset Aunt Faye. A debate ensued about the legalities, and to my surprise it was Lexie who sided with Duncan and I. When Bran had become annoyed that we hadn't had first contact with a Bishop descendant, it was Lexie who'd stopped his rant.

"Thomas Drake has the bankroll and the connections to locate Maggie and her child much faster than we ever could have," she told Bran. "What's done is done."

Aunt Faye began to argue that point, but it was Duncan who'd ended the discussion. "I'd like to remind you all," he said quietly. "Maggie Parrish is not only a Bishop descendant—she is also a Drake." His words were met with a ringing silence. "We have as much right to contact her as you."

"Boom," Ivy said, pantomiming the dropping of a microphone.

Holly covered her mouth to try and smother a laugh.

"Can we have dessert now?" Morgan asked.

"Yes," Lexie said, getting up from the table. "We can."

Dessert was served but no one really ate it. Afterwards, I left the photocopies with Bran, knowing he'd want to archive them with the other family papers. Aunt Faye had retreated to her room, Ivy and Nathan headed back to his apartment, and Holly had disappeared. Since Lexie and Bran were taking Morgan to a birthday party for one of his friends, I volunteered to babysit Belinda for a couple of hours.

Duncan carried the diaper bag, I hitched Belinda on my hip, and we walked back to the bungalow.

"Should I apologize for my family's reaction?" I said.

"No." He pulled the baby's hood up to protect her head from the cool breeze. "Give them a little time, Autumn," he suggested, as the wind stripped leaves from the trees.

I sighed. "I will."

Duncan went up the back porch steps and I handed him the door keys. "Remember, Thomas had a similar reaction, when he learned about Patricia." He unlocked the door and held it open for me and the baby.

As soon as we got inside, Belinda started to squawk and squeal. The five month old fussed as we took her sweater off. Duncan held her while I tucked a bottle in the fridge and set the diaper bag on the table. I fished out a few baby toys, and Duncan took the baby over to the couch and sat down with her in his lap.

I tried not to giggle as I walked over. Belinda was staring at Duncan, not sure what to make of him. I sat beside them and Belinda immediately reached out for me. I took her from Duncan and gave her a quick snuggle. "I don't know how Irene managed to give her baby up."

Duncan sighed. "I imagine she did what she thought was best."

While Belinda gnawed on her plastic baby keys, Duncan built a fire in the fireplace and turned on a football game. As soon as he sat down, I cuddled up and Luna leapt for the back of the sectional. The cat strolled over, arranging herself behind Duncan's head. It hit me hard in that moment that my life could be like this someday. Lazy Sunday afternoons with a fire in the fireplace, a football game on the television, and a baby in my lap.

"This is nice," I said.

Duncan kissed me. "It is."

Belinda yawned, and her head began to nod. Duncan tried to kiss me again and the baby started to fuss.

Before I could react, Duncan scooped her up. "Let me try something." He put the baby over his shoulder, and patted her back. "Take a snooze, Belinda," Duncan suggested.

I grinned at his smooth handling of the baby. "Well, look at you."

"I've seen Bran do this with her a few times. She's tired and wants to sleep, but is too wound up."

"You're reading her."

"It's not hard with babies." As if in agreement, Belinda rubbed her face tiredly against his shoulder. She wriggled around, but she soon settled in with a sigh. As Duncan patted her back, she curled up against him, and in a few moments she was out like a light.

"Do you want me to take her?" I asked softly.

"No." He smiled as my niece lay sleeping against his chest. Luna began to purr and Duncan settled in to watch his game.

Watching him with the baby had my heart melting. Sitting there with Duncan, I fingered the fluorite in my pocket, reinforced my protection so he wouldn't read my thoughts, and started to hatch a plan. Because if I hadn't figured out earlier that I was in love with him, seeing him holding Belinda would have certainly sealed the deal.

He'd be a wonderful father; caring, fun, and loving... I thought. *I didn't just love him. I wanted to marry him, and have kids.*

I wanted the faery tale. I wanted a happy ever after.

Now all I had to do was get him to propose. *Or I could be a modern woman,* I thought, *and tell Duncan that I loved him—and simply propose to him myself.*

At dinner.

Tonight.

I could make a fancy dinner...No scratch that. He'd know something was up. *I needed to try and play this cool.* "After Bran and Lexie pick up the baby would you mind running to the grocery store for me?" I said, going for a casual tone of voice. "I'll need a few things for dinner tonight. Avocados, fresh tomatoes, that sort of thing."

"Sure," Duncan answered, watching the game. "Are you going to make chicken fajitas? I love your chicken fajitas."

While Duncan focused on the football game I sat beside him and starting hatching how to pull off a romantic dinner, when I was only going to have a short time alone to prepare.

Lexie picked up Belinda right on time. She stopped short when she walked into the living room and found Belinda sitting happily on Duncan's lap.

Lexie slanted her eyes at me. "Have him practicing, already?" she said under her breath.

"He's been enjoying himself," I answered softly.

Lexie rolled her eyes. "Where's my monster?" she asked, and Belinda swung her head at her mother's voice and held out her arms.

After a few minutes Lexie and the baby returned to the manor, and I went into the kitchen to pull the chicken breasts out of the fridge. While Duncan watched the ending of his football game, I set the table and prepped the vegetables and chicken for cooking.

Having something to do with my hands helped keep me calm, and as I washed up in the sink I saw Irene's cookbook was out and on the counter once again. I glanced over at the cookbook as the pages started to flip, and had to muffle a snort of laughter when I saw that the recipe the book had landed on was: *Go Get Your Man Guacamole.*

I shook my head at her antics, briskly closed the book and tucked it back inside the cabinet. When the game was over, I handed Duncan a list of items. He gave me a quick kiss and promised he'd be back soon.

I held my breath until I saw him pull out of the driveway. I dashed upstairs and changed my clothes as fast as I could.

I tossed on a loose and flowing deep green maxi dress, fluffed my hair, touched up my makeup and sprayed on perfume. I slipped on a cute pair of flats and scrambled down the stairs, skidding to a halt when I saw that Irene was standing by the kitchen table.

"I added some candles," she said. "If you're going to propose to him, you need to set the mood, my girl."

I didn't have time to wonder how she'd known, or how she'd affected physical reality by moving the candle holders. "Thanks Irene," I said, as I dashed to the mantle and grabbed the lighter.

Sitting on the mantle was a framed photo that I hadn't displayed in years. It *had* been left in the box inside the closet. I studied the picture. It was a selfie that I'd taken of me and Duncan four years ago at the house I'd landscaped for him. "How long has this been out?" I asked Irene.

"I set it out for you, I thought it might help with the ambiance. Because, honestly Autumn," she huffed. "Chicken fajitas, as a romantic dinner?"

I went to the table and started lighting the candles. "Duncan *loves* my fajitas."

"Almost as much as your meatloaf?"

I started to glare at the ghost and found myself laughing instead. "Shut up, Irene."

She playfully wagged a finger at me. "I think you should definitely add *that* recipe to the family cookbook."

"Which reminds me." I dashed over, grabbed my

apron out of the drawer and tied it on to protect my dress. "How come most of the recipes in your cookbook have to do with love and sex?"

"Because that's what the clients typically requested the most."

I turned the heat on under the skillet. "You referred to them as *clients*?"

"Of course dear," Irene said. "They hired me out to perform a service, in this case magick, and I always did my best for them. Whether that was to offer metaphysical advice, brew a potion, work a spell, or—"

"Pass along a magickal recipe that they could cook for their partner."

"Precisely."

I pulled the chicken and diced peppers out of the fridge, peeled the plastic wrap off the bowl, and dumped it into the skillet. "Isn't that manipulation?"

"It was up to the client how they used the magick," Irene said. "I always explained the risks. It was up to them to decide *if* they wanted to proceed."

I checked the clock and stirred the chicken and peppers. "Like you did with Olivia's sister, Jane."

"That's right." Irene moved over next to me. "How are you feeling now, my dear? Are you calmer?"

"You've been staying with me, keeping me talking so I wouldn't be so nervous, haven't you?"

"Of course." Irene reached out, and I actually felt her rest a hand on my shoulder. "I promised Arthur, when you were an infant that I'd watch out for you."

I dropped the spatula, it clattered to the stovetop. "My father asked you to watch over me?"

"He did." Irene nodded. "Your father would have approved of Duncan, by the way. I thought you should know that."

Tears welled up and I struggled not to cry. "Thank you for telling me," I said sincerely. "Now do me a favor will you?"

"Of course."

"Make yourself scarce for the rest of the night."

"Done. Blessed be, dear." Irene winked and vanished.

The chicken and peppers were simmering when Duncan walked back in the door. "Smells great," he said, letting the door shut behind him. "The table is pretty fancy, what's the occasion?"

My stomach gave a good hard leap. "Does there have to be one?" I asked lightly.

"No." Duncan reached in the bag and pulled out a little bouquet of fall flowers. "No, there doesn't have to be any reason."

I leaned over and gave him a kiss. "Thank you, they're beautiful."

We worked side by side, with me arranging the flowers and Duncan chopping up the tomatoes and avocados. I set the flowers on the table, and Duncan placed the small bowls of the diced vegetables along with grated cheese and lettuce.

When the chicken was finished I slid it into a serving

bowl, Duncan carried it to the table, and I brought over the warm tortillas.

I tried to keep up with the conversation over dinner, and Luna sat under the table and lay on my feet. I wondered if she was trying to lend support, like a good familiar would. I struggled hard to hold my energetic shields in place, so Duncan wouldn't pick up on any stray thoughts.

I kept wondering when the perfect moment would be to tell him that I loved him. And how exactly should I propose? Say it straight out, or try and be romantic? Back and forth my mind went, and I was so nervous that I could feel beads of sweat running down my back.

Oh my goddess, I thought. *This is horrible. Do men suffer through all this when they plan to propose? Breaking out in a nervous sweat? Butterflies in the belly, and shaking hands? Maybe I should just say it and get it over with...*

"Should say what?" Duncan asked.

I could feel the blood drain from my face. "*What?*" I asked, horrified.

"You said, 'maybe I should just say it and get it over with'." Duncan tilted his head. "Something on your mind?"

"Ah..." I stammered. "Well, I was wondering...that is I wanted to tell you..." I caught myself rambling, and shut my eyes.

"Are you okay?" Duncan asked.

I opened my eyes and looked directly into his. "I

love you, and I was wondering...will you marry me?"

Duncan said nothing. He simply sat there while a big grin slowly spread over his face.

Nervously, I started talking. "I was thinking we could get married next year in a garden...The month of May would be a good for an outdoor ceremony."

He opened his mouth to speak, but I kept on going, speaking faster and faster. "We could have Candice make cakepops, and Violet would do our flowers...We'd have Lexie, Ivy and Holly as bridesmaids. I'd want a bunch of different colors though, all mixed together, in a rainbow of soft pastels..."

"Sounds like you've thought about this a little bit," Duncan said.

"Actually I saw it in a precognitive dream—the color scheme of our wedding," I tried to explain. "I didn't realize till a second ago, that *that's* what I'd seen. Kind of a Beltane theme...But anyway, afterwards. After the wedding, I mean, we could live here in the bungalow, and have a family. You said you were ready to have kids whenever I was. So...I'm ready."

"Right this second?"

His dry question had my mouth slamming shut.

"Well finally, you've wound down." Duncan rested his arms on the table. "If we could backtrack for a moment? Did you say that you loved me?"

I twisted my hands in my lap and tried not to get sick, or pass out. "I did."

"Took you long enough." His tone of voice was very

male, very satisfied.

I wasn't sure what to make of him, or his reaction. "I guess all this..." I waved my hands. "Babbling, sort of took you by surprise."

"You certainly manage to keep things interesting," Duncan said.

"I probably sounded like an idiot. Jabbering on about weddings when you haven't even answered my proposal." Mortified, I dropped my eyes to my lap.

"No you didn't sound like an idiot. It was adorable." Duncan lifted my chin with a gentle finger. He smiled. "You surprised me, that's all."

"I managed to surprise a telepath?"

He took my hands in his. "You sure as hell did."

I searched his eyes, and what I *saw* there made me smile. "I love you Duncan," I said deliberately.

"I love you, Autumn." Duncan leaned across the table and kissed me. "Yes, I will marry you." He kissed me a second time. "Yes, we can get married in May in a garden." He kissed me a third time. "Yes, I want to live here in the bungalow, and absolutely I want to start a family."

"Right this minute?" I teased him.

Duncan stood, scooped me up and carried me towards the stairs. "We can sure as hell practice making that baby—right now."

I laughed and wound my arms around his neck. "I really love you."

"I love you too," he said. "We can go shopping for a

ring tomorrow."

I kissed his neck as he went up the stairs. "Okay, I don't want a diamond though. I'd like something with color."

Duncan nudged the bedroom door open with his hip and carried me over to the bed. He set me gently on the quilt, and began unbuttoning his shirt. "I might have a little something in mind."

"Me too," I said, yanking him down to the bed.

He fell forward with a laugh. "I meant about the ring.

EPILOGUE

I stood unseen in the kitchen with the little calico familiar at my side, smiling at the couple as Duncan swept my great niece Autumn into his arms and carried her up the stairs and to the bedroom. I heard the couple's laughter drift down the stairs, and with a sentimental sigh, I wished them the happily ever after they so deserved. I focused my powers on the candles they'd left on the table, and one by one they snuffed out.

After years where I'd gone unnoticed, unheard and unacknowledged, the opportunity to help one of my own was indeed a magickal thing. I had watched, waited, and wandered the rooms of the bungalow, fading in and out for decades. I'd seemed to simply exist, stuck between the realm of spirit and the world of the living.

But the first time Autumn had walked back in the bungalow, I'd felt it. The magick had rekindled. My own bloodline had reignited the wards I'd managed to set on my last corporeal day on this earth.

For the first time in decades, I, Irene Bishop, had a purpose, and it had been very satisfying to help my great niece learn to trust, to love again, and to live her dream. It was the least I could do for her. Because now, thanks to Autumn and Duncan, my granddaughter and her child were coming back to William's Ford.

I had a few months to set things in motion for my Maggie. I actually had someone specific in mind for her, but for now I had to be patient. Once my girls were home and settled, I could begin to weave my magick, and then all the spells of the heart would be set right.

The End

Irene Bishop's granddaughter, Magnolia (Maggie)
Parrish is coming to William's Ford!
Turn the page for a sneak peek at Maggie's story!
Magick & Magnolias

Coming 2018

***

Magick & Magnolias

"Mama, are we there yet?"

I'd lost count of the number of times I'd heard that question over the past two days. Gripping the steering wheel tighter, I resisted the urge to scream. "No, sugar pie, we're not. But we're close."

"We are?" My daughter, Willow, bounced in her booster seat and I flashed my eyes to the review mirror in time to see her kick her snow boot clad feet in the air.

With relief I checked the GPS. "We should be arriving in less than a half hour." A massive double bridge came into view, and I counted five lanes heading west and five heading in the opposite direction. "See that bridge?" I desperately pointed out. "Once we cross that we'll be almost at our new house."

"Will I get to use my snow boots?" It was her second favorite question.

"I'm sure you will." I smiled when I said it, but internally I was thankful our trip up North had *not* included me driving through a snow storm—for the very first time.

"Can I see the pictures of our house, again?"

"Sure." I patted around, found my cell by touch and handed her my phone without taking my eyes off the road. With a terrifying skill she opened up the photo app and began to scroll through. "Do you see the pictures of the cottage?" I eased over in the far right lane of the bridge. Everyone was driving so fast, it was more than a little intimidating.

"Uh-huh. How come you don't have any pictures of Thomas?"

I thought back to the elegant older man who'd swooped in to our lives a few months before and saved the day. "Because he didn't send me any." It was the most honest thing I could think to say.

"Mama, I like our cousin. He's nice." Willow sang as she entertained herself looking at the pictures on my phone.

He certainly was, I thought to myself. Thomas Drake was also powerful, a little intimidating, and if every story that my mother had ever told me was true, the man was a magician as well. *Didn't that beat all?*

My mother Patricia had recounted a fantastical saga since I'd been a child, about how she was the secret love child of a Witch and a Magician. They'd given her up and had hidden her away, she'd said, to keep her safe. When I was little I'd been spellbound by the story, imagining my mother and me as some sort of secret princesses. But when I'd grown up I'd begun to roll my eyes at her tall tales, figuring that my mother was simply making up stories about her biological family for the entertainment value—or for attention.

So when I met her cousin Thomas, I wasn't sure what to think of the man. The older gentleman had carried himself with a sort of dignity, or polite arrogance I supposed. Truthfully, his wardrobe, fancy car, and bank account hadn't impressed me much. But copies of my mother's birth certificate and her adoption papers certainly had. In the short week he'd spent in town, he had humbled me with his quiet generosity, kindness, and sincere desire to help.

"You are my family," he'd said, and proceeded to steamroll his way through every obstacle that I had faced.

When all was said and done, he'd terrified my ex, found me an excellent realtor, and had hired the best damn attorney money could buy. Now my child was safe, my mother's house was sold, her medical bills were paid off from the sale, *and* I was free to get the hell out of Louisiana, and start my life over in Missouri.

Truth be told, I could work almost anywhere. As an event coordinator, or bridal consultant, I had that luxury. I'd built a solid reputation for myself in my hometown, I'd even landed some bigger events in Shreveport. I was pretty confident that I could do the same up North. My stomach gave a nasty pitch, and even as I told myself not to worry...I did anyway.

I took the first exit after crossing the bridge and, within moments, found myself driving through the river town of William's Ford, Missouri.

Picturesque, was the word that came first to mind, and thankfully the streets were dry and clear. I passed a smattering of restaurants, banks and stores. I spied two national chain pharmacies, a massive grocery store, and the University campus on my left.

The winter bare trees had a dusting of snow on their dark branches, and there was also a few inches on the grass. While Willow cheered over the snow, I admired the fancy decorative street lights along the roads. I cruised along with the local traffic, following the directions of the GPS. I rolled my shoulders against the tension gathered there, and drove into a gorgeous neighborhood filled with large Victorian era homes.

The brick sidewalks were also clear, and I slowed down, enjoying the view of the pretty homes and the large trees, trying to imagine what it would be like in the spring. I spotted the Drake mansion, stopped my car in the middle of the street, and sat there like a rube. "Lord mercy!"

The house really was a mansion. Three stories of gray stone, the huge house sprawled out impressively. The grounds of the estate were large, ensuring that no neighbors were particularly close—save one. Surrounded by trees, nestled a charming Tudor style cottage built from the same gray stone as the mansion.

"Willow, here's the cottage," I said, carefully easing into the driveway while my little girl cheered. I took a deep breath, blew it out slowly and told myself to stay calm.

My cell began to ring, and Willow answered it. "Hello?"

"Willow, give me the phone." I held out my hand.

"Hi Cousin Thomas!" Willow said. "We just got here. You have snow!"

How had he known we'd arrived? I wondered, then gave up waiting for her to give me back my phone. I shut off the engine and climbed out of the car. The cold was a shocking slap to the senses. *This Southern girl needs to thicken up her blood,* I thought. Reaching quickly for my new winter coat, I zipped it up. Willow was already unbuckling herself from the car seat, and I walked around to the passenger side of the car.

"Did you hang up?" I asked as she bounced out of the back seat.

"Cousin Thomas says he's coming over to help us settle in." Her breath made little white clouds against the January air. "Mama it's cold!"

"Yes, darlin' it is." I immediately tried to zip her coat. "Willow, stand still." I finally got the zipper pulled up, and as soon as I let go she took off for the nearest snow covered surface.

Willow entertained herself by jumping in a little pile of snow, and I retrieved my phone and purse. I grabbed Willow's backpack and shut the door, heading to the trunk for our bags.

"Hello," a male voice said. "You must be Magnolia and Willow."

I discovered a gorgeous, dark haired man. I estimated him to be in his early thirties. He walked through the snow wearing a navy overcoat, dark jeans and boots.

"Hi!" Willow ran past him. "I made footprints!"

"I'm your cousin, Julian." He smiled. "Thomas is my father."

"Hello Julian." I nodded, recalling that Thomas had given me a rundown on the current Drake family. "It's a pleasure to meet you."

He walked over and extended a hand. "It's lovely to finally meet you, Magnolia."

"Oh, honey please, call me Maggie." I automatically shook his hand. "Only my mama called me Magnolia." I looked up at his face and felt a jolt go all the way to my toes. My cousin's eyes were a startling combination of blue and brown. One eye had a ring of electric blue against the brown, and the other iris was brown with patches of that same bright blue color.

"Is something wrong?" he asked.

"Your eyes," I said, tugging him a bit closer. "Sectoral heterochromia." *I'd seen eyes like his before.*

"Hi cousin Thomas!" Willow launched herself at the older man. To my surprise he scooped her up and settled her on his hip.

"Hello Princess." Thomas gazed fondly at her. "How was your trip?"

"We drove forever!" Willow declared.

I finally remembered to release Julian's hand. "Well, I guess I got the answer to the question that's puzzled me for the past few years." I unlocked the trunk and raised it.

Julian cocked his head. "Oh, what question is that?"

"I'd always wondered where my daughter's unusual eye coloring came from." I gestured to where Thomas stood with Willow. "Now I have my answer."

Thomas walked up, and Julian glanced over at Willow. He narrowed his eyes for a moment, and slowly he began to grin.

Willow's right eye was blue, and her left was almost equally divided between both brown and sky blue colors.

"Her eyes are like mine." Julian sounded awed.

"It's a Drake family trait," Thomas said. "My uncle Phillip—your grandfather—he had the same mixture of eye colors."

"Funny old world, isn't it?" I put my hands on my hips as I looked from Julian to my daughter. For some reason, all the nerves that had been dancing in my belly smoothed out.

Julian laughed and tugged a suitcase from the trunk. "Welcome home, cousin."

***

Magick & Magnolias
Legacy Of Magick, Book #9
By Ellen Dugan
Coming 2018

***

28560478R00157

Made in the USA
Lexington, KY
17 January 2019